HIDING FROM MONSTERS

BLACKWOOD ACADEMY BOOK 1

K.J. THOMAS

Editor: Samantha Wiley

Proofreader: Rachel

Cover Artist: Thomas Moore Jr.

❀ Created with Vellum

To new changes...

CHAPTER 1

AVERY

Three Months Ago

My hands move uncontrollably as I pull the fleece blanket all the way up to my nose. I'm shaking so much, several times the blanket falls from my grasp. I remembered how it always made me feel safe as a child, hopefully now it keeps the demons away.

Deep down inside I know the demons are not going to stay away. The air around me is getting thick, making it hard to breathe. I can't stay in this position much longer, I've got to move.

In school, we learned when there's a fire stay low to the ground because heat rises. I'm crawling on my hands and knees trying to find my way through the thick cloud to the door.

The heat seems to close in on me from all directions, causing me to shiver and shake. Even though there's a huge inferno eating away at my child-hood home, for some reason I'm extremely cold.

I only have on my camisole and a pair of boy shorts, *God, where are my parents?*

It takes me at least a few minutes to get through a coughing attack, they're coming more sporadically now. It's hard to crawl when I'm trying to cover my face with the top part of my camisole, the fumes and the smoke are so thick. A couple of loose tears escape, cleaning the black soot from my face, leaving a trail.

"No," I stop dead in my tracks as I hear a scream coming from my mom. Oh God, I think as I crawl faster back over to my bed not even caring if my mouth and nose are covered.

It only takes five seconds for me to find my phone, which is what I should have done in the first damn place. I quickly place a call to the 911 operator and croak out, "fire," when they answer.

The phone falls from my hands as I curl on my side. All I want to do is sleep, but I realize if I do fall asleep, I won't be getting back up. If I stay on the floor, I will die.

The smoke is thick, making it impossible to see or breathe, I don't have much time. The phone case shimmers from the fire that's not far away. I grab my dropped phone and crawl for my window, violently yanking the thing open.

All of the movies and T.V. shows I've seen people in, show that they're going to get a refreshing gush of fresh air when they get a window open, but that's not happening here. The acid in the air and the thick fumes form a black cloud chasing after me, pushing out the window just like I'm doing, making it impossible for me to find a good breath.

My windowsill has a tiny ledge enough for me to get out on. Unfortunately, my bedroom happens to be located on the third floor.

With shaky hands and legs, I manage to crawl out. I spend what seems like hours gasping in a lung full of clean air, but it was probably only seconds.

The smell is horrendous, like I'm sucking in acid that's burning the sensitive tissue allowing me to breathe. The taste is so much worse. My dad would BBQ a lot, he would BBQ every night if my mother would let him. That's what the taste reminds me of, licking a hot BBQ.

I can hear the sirens heading to our estate, far away but coming, we're located in a richer area of Chicago.

My parents' room is only three doors down, so three windows down on the ledge. Their room is dark, I don't see any movement. *Where was my mom, where did she scream from?*

I start to frantically look around, there has got to be a way down or maybe I can get into another window. Out of the corner of my eye, movement grabs my attention, around the garage like someone's watching.

My breath catches and tears spring free, it only takes me seconds to figure out who it is. Luca, my ex-boyfriend that I just broke up with a few hours ago. "Did he start this?" I whisper to myself. He had to, he's not helping just watching the show.

I try to bend down a little bit to hide, pressing myself as much as I can against the wall. If Luca did start this then he's intending to get rid of all of us. What if he sees me, will he shoot me? I know he always carries a gun and

I know he's not a good man, he never was. Once I realized this it was hard to get away from him.

Luca still has his focus on the fiery blaze that was my house, he doesn't even notice me.

I don't know how long I can stand out here. I'm standing on my tiptoes and my fingers are starting to turn white from the strain of holding onto the windowsill.

The dark night lights up with the red and blue lights of rescue workers. "Thank God," I say softly as the tears start to roll down my face. *Please let my parents be okay, please,* I repeat to myself multiple times.

Keeping my eyes trained on him, he still hasn't spotted me as he notices all the rescue workers pulling into the gate.

We have another gate that's located off the back side of the property. That's where he's heading as he jumps into his car moving in that direction.

I watch the whole thing unfold. Eventually my fumed-out brain kicks in and I wave my arms frantically towards the rescue workers that haven't seen me yet. I want them to go through the rest of the house first. What if they don't even know that my parents are in the house?

Screaming at the top of my lungs waving only one hand at a time, holding on for dear life with the other. I don't know if a three-story fall will kill me, but I'm not gonna chance it. They finally spot me as a ladder is hoisted up to get me from the window.

I wave it away and start to scream. "My parents," as I point my finger towards their room, hoping that they're safely outside.

My voice cracks on deaf ears as the ladder continues to hoist up towards me.

Within a minute I'm back on the ground as they finally go to that window that I was pointing to.

I run over to the man that looks to be in charge and grab his jacket forcing him to focus his attention on me. "My parents, I heard my mom scream earlier somewhere in the house, please."

The middle-aged man with a slight dusting of gray that peeks out from underneath his helmet gives me a sad smile. "We're doing everything we can now, miss, I need you to step over into that area," He says in a small reassuring voice, as he points over to a grassy area far away from any buildings.

I realize I'm not letting this guy do his job, so I move over to a grassy patch that we have that's closer to the gate and far away from the house.

I don't even know what else to do now, I just sit defeated letting the tears fall. They don't just fall, they gush out, leaving me drained of all bodily fluids.

———

I DIDN'T SAY ANYTHING AS THEY LOADED ME INTO AN ambulance and drove me to the hospital. I can't, my brain just isn't working right now.

As I'm given a full checkup, people try to talk to me. I ignore everyone, I don't want to even try to pretend to talk back.

My parents are dead. That's the last thought I have before I pass out.

I am grateful to the nurses and the doctor. I'm not exactly sure what they did or what they gave me, but it knocked me out. If sleep is the only escape I can have now, then so be it.

MY NERVES ARE ON EDGE AND I CAN'T SIT IN THIS ROOM anymore and wait for night time to finally arrive so I can go back to sleep. I make my way through the hospital to the cafeteria. There are officers everywhere, adorning different types of uniforms from different agencies. I was able to spot the FBI, the Chicago Police Department and even a crime scene unit. I know they're more agencies. I think one of them was DEA, but I stopped looking after I started wondering what the hell's going on.

We're not royalty and from all the people here, you would think a major catastrophe happened. At first I thought they were here for something else, but most of them keep giving me pity smiles. Some of them look annoyed with me. No other patients or visitors are allowed to be in the same place I am. Men watch the entrance to the cafeteria, only allowing in staff and essential workers.

A man whom I've never seen before, sits across from me as I sip on my juice. I should feel creeped out and annoyed, but I just don't care. There is something familiar about him. He's older with graying hair, but we share the same green eyes.

He gives me a tight smile in understanding and then just blurts out, "your parents were murdered tonight."

"What?" I stammer as I start to look between him and the cops. I don't want to believe him, but I already know this is true.

One day in the future I'll remember as he didn't give an answer when he held me as I cried for the loss of my parents.

I watch as cops bring us both a cup of coffee. Another one comes over and looks at the kind stranger, waiting for orders and he gives a nod, then she takes off the way she came.

The pain is unbearable. My parents were definitely not perfect, but they're still my parents and they were good people, they did the best they could, and I know they loved me.

"What happened?" I ask on a whimper. Before he gets a chance to answer, I continue, "who are you?"

The man who resembles my mother takes a deep breath and then slowly lets it escape as he says, "it was Luca."

My mouth opens wide. Luca Delano is the son of another huge crime family. Our families thought it would be great when we got together. We needed a truce, and nothing like young love to do that. Only mine didn't realize how crazy Luca was and how obsessive he would become of me.

I tried at first to explain to him that he was so much better than me. He laughed at me and said he would never let me go. I have to say that was the first time that I was actually nervous that something bad could happen between us.

After a while, the family started getting involved. My

parents called his parents and told them to take control of their son, which they thought his parents did.

My parents were very vocal with him. Dad warned and threatened him, he even blocked him from contacting me. A sob forces its way out as I realize that he killed them thinking that we would be able to be together now, or maybe he also wanted me dead.

I knew it was Luca, but hearing it said out loud by someone else, makes it a reality.

Two men in similar suits walk up to us. One looks to be in his fifties and the other one looks to be in his thirties. They both look like they've been obsessed with donuts every day of their career.

"Mr. Romano, we really feel it's imperative that you give some thought to the witness protection program."

For the first time tonight, the man sitting next to me laughs, but it doesn't reach his eyes as he looks at them.

"There is no fucking way I'm putting my granddaughter in your hands again. This time the family will take care of it," he snaps out his answer to them. *Granddaughter?* My mother told me my grandpa died years ago.

I snap my head in his direction. 'The family will take care of it', does that mean they're going to go kill him now?

"I will be sending my granddaughter, my last living heiress relative to live with family. No, I will not tell anybody where she's going and that includes you idiots."

It's quiet for a second, all of the cops and other agencies stop doing what they're doing and watch my grandfather.

"Sir, we don't recommend that idea." The older detective spits out at him. The detective is starting to get angry or maybe he's just annoyed that he has to be here in the first place.

"Didn't ask you. If you have a problem with it, you can take it up with Judge Michaelson." I've heard that name before, my parents often mentioned him, and the look on the officers faces suggest that they've heard it before also.

Does my newfound grandpa have a judge on the payroll? Probably.

The suits eventually give up and walk away, leaving me alone with my grandfather again. The silence is extremely uncomfortable, but I know he's processing this as much as I am. I might have lost my parents, but he lost his daughter, *my mom.*

The tears fall down uncontrollably again as the officer from earlier returns holding shopping bags, with what looks to be all new clothes and toiletries. Everything I owned is most likely gone now.

I looked over at my grandfather and asked. "Where are we going? Will I be back in time for my senior year?"

He gives me a sad smile and shakes his head, turning around to make sure that nobody is close or eaves-dropping. "Your mother has a cousin in Northern California, my niece, that you'll be staying with. We were able to transfer you to Blackwood Academy." It's a great school, but not the one I had my heart set on. Blackwood has been on the news repeatedly, but for only good things. I think the president went there.

Right now, I don't want to feel anything, so I don't ask questions. I might not know this man very much, but I trust him. It's nice to let someone else take control for a while. All I want to do is curl up in a ball and sleep for a week. Maybe the tears will stop, and my heart will quit painfully squeezing by the time I wake up.

"Are you coming?" I sit up a little straighter with my eyes wide.

"No dear, I'm sorry, but you will be very well taken care of. I need to stay here to end this. Wherever I am, they're going to think you're with me. This is the safest thing for you *mia bella*."

I never knew we had family on the west coast. Something must have happened with my mom's cousin for her to never be mentioned. Maybe it was my mom all along, she never mentioned my grandfather, either. I want to ask questions, but my heart won't let me, that is for another time.

Grandpa gets the attention of a couple of guards standing by the door. I know their names are Tony and Marco, they've been with the family for years. I really like them, they've always been nice to me. I wonder if they knew my grandfather was alive.

They both come over as one of them grabs my shopping bags, giving me a sad smile.

Grabbing my hand, my grandfather speaks in a soft tone, "I have the family plane ready to take you to California, you are leaving now. The farther away you are from here, the safer you are."

I shake my head no, I feel like I'm twelve years old all over again. I don't wait for permission as I wrap my arms around his neck. "I don't want to leave without you, please, you're all I have left."

A tear escapes from my grandpa's eye and trails down

his cheek, he quickly wipes it away. Even though he's trying to be strong for me, a man of his position can never show weakness, even to your loyal guards.

"It won't be for long. As soon as everything is safe and the Delano's are dealt with, then we'll be reunited." His voice sounds more choked up.

I nod my head in understanding, I knew exactly what he meant. It's an old family tradition. Luca went too far, so basically the whole family is going to have to pay for everything now. The Romano's will take out all of them. I should feel bad, a lot of people over there are going to lose their lives for what Luca did, but I don't. Their son was a psychopath and they did nothing about it, so they all deserve it. "Not Gabe though, right?" My grandfather, whom I'm starting to realize is the head of the Romano family, just gives a sad smile and doesn't say anything.

Gabriel Delano is Luca's younger brother, he has been nothing but nice to me the whole time I've known him. I can't tell my grandfather what to do, but I can reach out to Gabe, giving him notice and hopefully allowing him to escape. I don't give a shit about the rest of the Delano's, they deserve what's coming to them.

My grandfather finally relents and rides with me to the airport. Not once did I ever take my hand out of his. I have so many questions I need answers to, but from the look on his face, now is not the time, hopefully my mom's cousin will have more information for me.

He kisses me on the forehead and says, "you'll be alright, *mia bella*, just don't bring attention to yourself and stay hidden."

"I know." I know what he's asking of me and I have no

choice. The car door shuts as the driver pulls away with my grandfather in the backseat and I'm loaded onto an airplane ready to take me to my new destination.

It's not the final place in my book, it's just one of the middle chapters.

CHAPTER 2

ASHER

Present

The annoying creak of the door opening snaps my attention to the right. Doppler, my guard isn't patiently waiting for me to get out, *fucker*.

I have a few choice words I would like to share with the steroid ass, but now is not the time. I squint my eyes at him knowingly as he smirks back.

Liam steps out right behind me, passing me my suit jacket. I take several seconds longer than needed to put it on. I want to scan the area around me. I have highly trained men protecting me, but you never know when a rival could slip through. I pay them all a shit ton of money to make sure I'm okay, but the only person who's going to take care of me, is me.

My guard is up as I take in every noticeable object on the streets. My mind plays every scenario possible on repeat. I'm continuously looking for threats. I have ten men with me but that doesn't mean shit.

Buttoning my Armani suit jacket, I look around. Most people won't look me in the eye. We're on a New York sidewalk getting ready to enter a fancy restaurant whose food is going to be toddler sized and overpriced. I'd rather go to the little Italian bistro right by the family estate.

I didn't set up this meeting, and I don't know the area very well, so I am more cautious than normal. I walk with my men flanking me. Fathers pull their families closer, shielding them. One lady grabs her two children by the hand and quickly walks away in the opposite direction.

I guess my reputation precedes me.

There are only a few that dare to smirk or look in my direction. In all honesty those are the ones that I respect the most. Of course, these are pre-teenage boys and gold-digging women.

A shiver runs through me, not from fear but from the cold air. We are in the upper east side of Manhattan, a place I loathe. I have more money than all these fake fuckers but being around them makes my skin crawl.

The maître d' comes to the door to open it for us. The big smile on his face quickly falters as he gets a glimpse of me and my men. I don't bother saying anything. I walk by not paying him a second glance. Even if I wanted to be nice, which I don't, I can't. I have a reputation to maintain and fear to evoke. The other families are always trying to get rid of me. I don't have the patience for that shit again, and if I'm not an asshole, I'm a target. My age doesn't help my situation, either. I'm an adult but just barely, and all these assholes think they'll pull one over on me, even when they've heard the rumors of what I can do to those that want to betray me.

The restaurant smells just as I would expect it to, fancy and boring. Don't get me wrong, sometimes I love boring, but boring can mean more surprises if your body relaxes.

My men did a thoroughly good job getting the blueprints and going through every fine detail to find out any areas that are inaccessible or easy to hide.

Younger women always parade around me. They put on their sexy ass smiles and walk towards me ready to pounce. Bitches will never learn, they should know when I'm ready, I'll choose. I don't even care if she is happily married, no woman has refused me. I unnoticeably shake my head. If I didn't know me and heard the shit that just came out of my mouth, I would think my head and ego are too big and my dick too small.

Including the one walking towards me right now. I can't tell what's real on this girl, most of it looks fake. She's stick thin with boobs that had to cost some poor bastard a shit ton of money. Her facial features don't look natural, just unhealthy.

"Mr. Mancini," she purrs as she waves her hand behind her. "Let me show you to your table, the other party has already arrived."

I narrow my eyes at her, not even responding she gets the message, she turns and leads the way. I follow behind looking everywhere and anywhere in the restaurant.

They're all set up the same, beautiful wooden tables with white, brighter than anything, tablecloths draped over the top.

Most of the people here are elderly or screaming of money, but older. One table I pass by has an uncomfortable looking girl, in too tight of a dress. *Date night*. Her date is older than my grandfather.

I shake my head as I walk up to my intended table. Alfonso Paluzzi stands up and gives me a firm shake of his hand. Maybe it's just a guy thing but I give it back twice as hard. I can see his eyes crinkle for a split-second.

"Asher, it's been so long, we shouldn't have to meet like this." I raise my brow, little fucker has a lot of nerve.

"Please, please, sit down," he says. Alfonso looks like he's in his forties, his hair is starting to recede, and he smells like desperation and body odor.

When I looked him up, he was only in his early thirties. Stress and diet has not done him any favors in the aging process.

As soon as we take our seats the waiter quickly makes his way towards us. I shake my head. I'm hungry, but not for this shit.

Alfonso quickly shoos him away and pours us both a glass of wine. Fucker must be stupid if he thinks I'm going to take a drink. I don't drink anything unless it's prepared by somebody I trust or something I've gotten myself.

My family and all of its members are one of the most wanted families in the country by the government, feds, cops, CIA and by all of the rival families. I have to be very vigilant in everything I do. One little lapse in judgment, means the end of me. One of my idiot nephews would have to take over the business. I sigh inwardly when I think of my nephews and my niece.

"What can I do to make this right with you?" Fatty interrupts me out of my thoughts.

"Two million dollars, plus twenty percent interest for

wasting my fucking time." His eyes go wide as he stares in disbelief.

Some of the Paluzzi men decided they would take one of the Mancini shipments. Their plan was that I wouldn't find out or I'd blame some other high-ranking family. That didn't work out that well for them. When I questioned them, they sang like a bird. Everyone involved has been taken out, not by me, but by my men.

We probably saved half of the shipment worth a million dollars, but the Paluzzi's need to learn a lesson.

"I can't afford that," the bitch states as he starts to freak out. If I could've, I would've killed him already. I can't stand this fucker, but keeping with the family code, we only go after who deserves it through the eyes of the families. We never mess with women or children unless absolutely necessary, but sometimes we've had to take them out just to get the attention of the dumbasses. Everyone knows how we feel on this subject, but nobody's willing to try and see if we'll actually do something. I would like to say that we wouldn't, but business is business.

"You have until five pm today, or we come after all of you." Alfonso's face turns beet red, letting me know he got my message.

I start to stand up and straighten out my jacket. My father always taught me to be the best dressed person in there. Respect is earned different ways. Everyone respected my father, and people don't fuck with me, either.

Out of the corner of my eye I see Alfonso nod to a couple of his guys behind me. I groan inwardly, because

I'm going to have to deal with this in a public fucking restaurant. At least we're in a private area way in the back.

I glance to Doppler twenty feet away letting him know some shit's about to go down. The eight guards that are in the restaurant with us quickly jump up and head in our direction, with Doppler in the front. I twist around fast and smack the knife out of the hand of one of Alfonso's men as he lunges for me. With my right hand I punch the bitch square in the throat.

"Fuck," I yell, not paying attention to the other guy that's still heading my way. Blood droplets spray over my five-thousand-dollar suit, as one of my men shoot him right in the forehead. "Well this one's going in the trash," I mumble under my breath.

Out of the corner of my eye I spot the beefy guy as he launches himself towards my upper body. I quickly kneel down letting him grab as much air as he wants.

My men catch up and are able to restrain Alfonso's men quickly.

"Please, please, please. That shouldn't have happened. I don't even know what I was thinking. I haven't been in the right frame of mind, just don't hurt me."

I look at Doppler and give a nod as I grab a napkin off the table and start to dab my suit. "Fuck, this is useless," I say as I watch Doppler drag Alfonso away. This will be the last time anybody sees him alive.

His screaming is quickly silenced, one of my men must've put him in a chokehold, knocking him out.

Doppler hands the man over to one of my other guys, as the maître d' shows us out through the back door. In New York, these restaurants deal with this shit all the time. From my understanding another higher up family, maybe the Irish or the Russians, own this restaurant. I'm not sure and honestly, I don't even give a shit. The people who work here just know not to fuck with us.

New York has gotten colder since we've been inside. Breathing in through my mouth lets me know of the weather that's coming.

I've heard people talk a lot about how an injury lets them know when the weather will change. Old joints and scar tissue, whatever it may be, they are the true weatherman. I've been shot and stabbed multiple times and I still have none of that. I even broke my kneecap. Well, I didn't break it per se, the bitch that kicked it in broke it. My shit doesn't flare up when cold weather is coming.

"Are we still going to make the flight?" I look over at Liam, then back over to Doppler. I nod to answer Liam's question and to make things easier on Doppler knowing our plans.

My niece has been going to school at Blackwood Academy in Northern California. Only a few members of our family know that I start my senior year there in three months. For family reasons I had to skip a year, but now I'm determined to get it done. I don't need to get my diploma, but I want it. I've invested too many years in school to stop now. I'd rather finish my diploma in New York, but a change of scenery is always welcomed.

My main focus isn't just getting my diploma, I'm hoping to find a reprieve from my daily life. I can't wait to see the look on Tatum's face when she realizes I'm going to the same school as her. Being the head of the family, she still has to show me respect, even though she's only a year younger than I am. I doubt if that'll be a problem, it's her brother's she can't stand.

"Let's go to the airport now." I just want to get this over with. "Make sure there's a car waiting for us when we land at SFO." I start to change into a new suit that Doppler grabbed from the trunk for me. I won't be caught dead in this filthy shit.

"Make sure that no one knows we're on our way. I don't want Tatum to know we're coming."

"Got it boss," Liam says as he quickly starts typing on his phone.

I've got at least fifty minutes till we arrive at the airport. I close my eyes; fresh clothes and a nap should clear my head.

CHAPTER 3

AVERY

I take a deep breath after I exit the diner where I work, nothing can beat the fresh air walking to the only friend's house that I've made since being in California.

My family didn't want me to get a job at the diner, but what else was I supposed to do? I only know three people in California, and I am bored out of my mind. At least I feel like I'm contributing at the diner. I even buy the groceries at the house, I don't have enough to help out with the bills, but at least I can do something.

I don't have to walk but this is the one time I have to myself that I enjoy. It's peaceful and it's only five minutes from Tate's house.

The streets are starting to get empty, maybe because it's a Sunday night and it just started getting dark. Nobody wants to be out, everyone wants to be in bed preparing for work tomorrow. College classes haven't even started yet.

My full name is Mila Avery Romano. I've always gone

by Avery, my mom's cousin's last name is Stone, so that's what I use, Avery Stone.

I wipe away a stray tear that slides down my cheek and shake my head, I miss my parents so much. I've been taught to show no weakness. Life could be so much better for me, but then life could be a hell of a lot worse.

I'm so lost in my thoughts that I don't even realize the two men that step-in front of me as I smash right into one. The smell of alcohol, body odor and cigarettes are overwhelming. It makes me scrunch my nose and step back.

They both give me evil smirks telling me what they're up to. I groan inwardly, not in the mood to do this shit tonight. Who the fuck tries to rob somebody on a Sunday night?

I chuckle to myself when they start to push me into the alley I was walking by. I should probably run or fight, but I got nothing else to do and they ruined my good vibes on my relaxing walk.

I feel a little sad for their parents when I glance at both of them, they both have blue eyes and are almost the same height but they're really thin and their clothes are extremely dirty. They look like college students that have gone the wrong way. Instead of hitting the books, they hit the bad shit.

'So sad,' I shake my head keeping the words to myself. They both look between me and each other wondering why I'm not scared.

It's time to get this over with, I think, as I go to lift my hand. At the same time my phone rings, of course.

"Just a minute," I say. Both of their eyes bug out, maybe they think I'm fucking crazy. I've been told that before.

"Hello," I answer as happily as I can.

"Avery," Tatum says in a whisper.

"What's wrong with you? Why are you talking so weird?" One of the men starts to move closer to me showing me that he's got a six-inch blade. I hold my palm straight out to him, making sure he gets the message and backs the fuck off.

He stumbles for a second and then I turn my head back to my conversation.

"Nothing's wrong. I just need you to do me a favor and take your time coming over. I'll call you when it's okay." Tatum whispers again. I can hear the fear in her voice.

"What the fuck is going on?" I snap out.

"Nothing, please stay away for a little bit." Tate quickly hangs up the phone ending our conversation.

I pocket my phone and swing back to look at the guys, still not fully concentrating on them. "What the fuck is going on?" I say to no one in particular.

One of the guys finally grows a set of balls as he says, "you're being robbed."

I laugh. "I don't have time for this shit," I say as the man moves closer, waving the knife.

Years of training has prepared me for this. My parents wanted me to be prepared for anything, these two are a joke. I kick his hand, noticing that he's not holding the knife tight. The blade starts to twirl in the air. While he's concentrating on the knife, I clock him right in the face.

It looks like the knife is twirling in the air in slow motion as I reach out and grab the handle.

The only thing that sucked was the exercise that accompanied the training. I honestly believe this is still why I hate exercise so much. My parents started having me trained when I was a toddler. They didn't want to take any chances because of the family business and who my grandfather is. I thought he was dead this whole time. I never got to ask him if he knows why they lied. That is at the top of my list of questions next time I see him.

Who knows how long that'll take, revenge can take a while. He did give me his phone number, with a promise I wouldn't call him unless it was an absolute emergency. He was afraid I would be tracked.

"You guys should really get off drugs," I say as I flash the shiny blade between both of them. Their mouth and eyes are wide open. I can't tell with all the drugs they're on and the scars covering their faces exactly how old they are.

I jump an inch in their direction, they both flinch but the response time is slow. It takes a second before they gather their wits and run the opposite way.

I still don't have time for this, I need to get back and figure out what the hell's going on. Why my roommate and best friend of years doesn't want me to come over. Did something happen to her or is somebody messing with her? Who the fuck knows.

I watch as the idiots run away and shake my head. I wish I had more time to teach them a lesson. Maybe I could kick the shit out of them or drive their asses down to jail. That would look funny, a hundred and ten-pound woman dragging two guys taller than her to the jail house.

They would be the laughing-stock of the whole building, shit, of the whole town.

I throw the knife in a nearby dumpster, then I take off in a slight jog towards Tate's. I want to get there as fast as I can. I loathe any form of exercise: running, cardio, anything except for walking.

I'm one of those people that only run when being chased, but I need to get somewhere fast and someone I love is in trouble.

I wave to Tate's elderly neighbor, Mrs. Williams, as I jog by. She looks behind me, probably to see if I'm being chased by anything.

She relaxes and gives me a nod with a sweet smile back. She's just the sweetest little old woman. I wipe the thoughts from my head, it makes me think of my family. I don't need the waterworks to show up now.

The stomping on the staircase inside the foyer lets me know that at least several people are coming down. Distracting me from the several vehicles in the circular driveway. I slow to a walk and look up. Nobody should be up here unless they're here for us.

Holding tightly to the handrail I make my way up the stairs to Tate's room. My eyes look up and my body leans back. I'm not one to be intimidated that much but there's got to be at least eight to ten men walking down the staircase, and all of them are dressed to the nines.

They all have on dark, almost black, tailored suits. The ones I can see look like they're fucking exercise junkies.

Don't even get me started on the loafers, I don't see a scuff mark on them.

They all walk down the stairs on the other side of me.

Every time one of them walks by their jacket or part of their pant leg brushes against me. This wouldn't have happened if they leaned against the side like I am. These guys aren't considerate, not even for little ol' me.

My eyes focus on the one that's in a light gray suit. He looks just as big, if not bigger, than the other ones. The suit fits exceptionally well on this guy, and he exudes confidence. It makes me gasp. Normally people don't scare me, but this man is intimidating as fuck.

When he starts to pass down towards me, he never takes his dark blue eyes off mine. I shudder and he smiles. He can tell what he does to me. He's close enough to where I can smell him, and his scent is intoxicating, woodsy and citrus, all male.

I'm not one to blush, but fuck if I don't feel that shit all over my face right now.

I don't pay as much attention to the men that are coming down after him, they're dressed the same as the ones before. I turn and focus my attention on the guy that just walked by. He does manage to turn around once more and give me a glare. *Why is he glaring at me?*

None of the other men turn back to look as they reach their vehicles. Not that it matters, the one who grabbed my attention was the one in gray. Another man, bigger than the guy I've been ogling, ushers everyone in the black SUV's quickly. This guy is Japanese and just as gorgeous as the rest.

"Holy shit," I whisper. I need to shake myself out of my stupor. My hormones are flowing a little bit too high right now.

I run up the stairs and bust into the house like I'm the

actual fucking police. I'm in panic mode right now, I need to find my best friend.

For a brief second, I thought the Delano's found me and were here for me. But this group of men looks too sophisticated to be Luca's family, plus the fact that they didn't even acknowledge me.

It's bad enough having a murderous family come look for you, it'll be even worse letting a possible rival family know who you are. The only people who know who I am in this state are me, my mom's cousin, and her husband. I plan to keep it this way, no one can find out who I am.

Whimpering pulls me out of my thoughts, I follow the noise to the kitchen area, spotting my friend on the floor with her head planted on her knees, sobbing.

"Tate," I say in shock as I run over and sit down next to her.

She looks up at me with her eyes wide open and then has the audacity to ask, "are you okay?"

"What the fuck are you talking about?" I wave between her and me. "You're the one on the floor crying. Why wouldn't I be okay?"

"D-did you pass them?" She asks on a stutter.

Grabbing my hand, she waits for my answer. "Yeah the hot guys that went down the stairs."

"Did they do anything to you?" She squeezes my hand a little too tight, which I quickly yank away.

"No, they didn't do anything," *which is too bad*. I focus my attention back on Tate. "What the hell is going on?"

Tate sighs as she gets up and wipes the tears from her eyes. My best friend is a gorgeous girl, she's the same age as me, seventeen, but a couple inches shorter than I am.

Her blue eyes glisten from all the tears making them look green.

Tate makes her way over to the cabinet where her parents keep the good shit. She pulls out a couple wine glasses and an expensive bottle of whiskey.

"That was my uncle and his minions, Asher Mancini."

I freeze, I was not expecting that. The Mancini's are a huge crime family out on the east coast and the only reason I know this is because I'm from Chicago. They're based in New York, but they have their finger in everything illegal and legal on the east coast.

"Holy shit, you're a Mancini?"

Tate takes a huge drink and then passes me a glass. I do the same waiting for her to continue. "My real name is Tatum Mancini, and I'm so sorry I didn't tell you Avery."

I take another drink and look at her, "I'm shocked, but I can understand." If she only knew how much I understood.

"Asher said I had to go back, Avery."

I snap at her. "What do mean, you got to go back?"

"I left home before my junior year ended. I changed my last name to Connor hoping that they wouldn't find me, but it sounds like Asher knew where I was the whole time. He says it's time for me to come home." Tate starts to cry again, "God, our senior year is just starting."

"Maybe you could just talk to him, he seemed like he was nice."

Tate shakes her head, "He is not nice, and neither is the rest of my family. Except for one of my brother's, but there is nothing he can do to help me. My other brother's will beat the shit out of me for leaving once I get back."

"Holy fuck, Tate. What the hell is wrong with your family?" Probably the same thing that's wrong with all of the families, I think to myself.

We both sit in silence for a few minutes. "I'm going to have to leave." She talks so low I almost didn't hear her.

"No," I say as I squeeze her hand. "I'm pretty good at reading people." *No, I'm not,* I whisper to myself. "Asher looks like a nice enough guy, just talk to him."

Tate spits out the drink she had had. "There's no talking to Asher Mancini. He's the head of the family, he didn't get this way by being nice."

I think for a few more seconds and ask, "honestly, if he said you had to go back right away, why are you still here?"

My friend sighs and chugs down the rest of her drink. "He said he had some work to do but will be back."

I start to pace, there's got to be something we can do. "We can figure this out, but holy fuck," I look back at my best friend, "you're a fucking Mancini."

"It's not something I'm proud of, it's something I wish I wasn't."

In my heart I know it would be the perfect time for me to open up to her to tell her everything about my past life, but I can't do it.

We finish off the bottle, then I help a slobbering Tate into her room. Her eyes will be swollen tomorrow from crying.

I make sure the house is locked up good. I doubt it'll keep the Mancini's out, but it makes me feel better.

I make my way back up to Tate's room and lay down on the bed next to my passed-out friend. Her mouth is

29

open and scrunched up in a funny position. I want to snap a picture, but this night is not something worth remembering.

The alcohol is rapidly coursing through my veins as I start my research on the Mancini's. I only lasted a few minutes before I pass out, face down on my phone.

CHAPTER 4

AVERY

I roll on my back, everything feels so good that I don't want to wake up from this awesome dream I'm having.

I can feel the trail of a callused-finger running down the side of my cheek. On instinct my body tries to gravitate closer towards the warm feeling of being touched.

I moan before it hits my brain receptors that I'm being touched, and I'm staying the night at my friend's house.

My eyes fly open as I take in my surroundings. I fill my lungs getting ready to scream.

"No, no, no, *mon cher.*" A velvety voice whispers over my skin. The warm breath right by my ear causes a massive case of goosebumps.

It's dark but there's a little bit of moonlight coming in through the curtains, letting me make out the unidentified stranger. It takes me a few seconds, but I can eventually see that it's Asher Mancini.

Why the fuck is he here? God, is he going to kill me? Did something happen to Tate?

My brain pushes my body into action as I try to leap from the bed. Asher softly laughs and wraps his arms around me pulling me onto his lap with his hands still covering my mouth.

I look to my side seeing that my best friend is still passed out and snoring through all the racket. She is such a lightweight when it comes to alcohol.

"Relax, nobody's going to hurt you," he purrs into my ear. "I'll release my hand over your mouth if you promise to be a good girl."

I try to say yes, but my mouth is covered. I roll my eyes and nod my head. At least I'm starting to wake up now. I might have a chance of getting out of this. Just from what I've heard, you never should trust a Mancini.

I started researching them last night, but I must have fallen asleep.

Asher releases his hand over my mouth, and I stay true to my word and keep it shut. My left arm isn't being held and I'm about ready to clock him on the side of the head, when I spot movement coming from the far side of the room. I can barely make out their shadows, but there's two more guys in the room with us, these must be guards.

Fuck, I'm not a bad fighter, actually rather good from what my trainers have told me. I don't know if I can take out three guys, plus who knows if there's any more hiding in the little dark corners of Tate's room.

If they wanted Tate, they would've already grabbed her, they're probably here to kill me. I start to shake a little, getting more frightened. My fight or flight instinct has grabbed hold and is shaking the shit out of me telling me to get my ass in gear.

"Relax," Asher says sternly, almost on a growl, "we are not here to hurt you."

He lifts me ever so sweetly off his lap and puts me where we're sitting face-to-face.

"I just wanted to thank you, Avery." He says as he lets my name roll off his tongue. His fingers wipe away a strand of hair that got stuck to my lip. "You've been there for my niece. Stupid girl if she only knew what could've happened to her." He looks down at me, deep in thought. "I find it ironic that the guards I had stationed here never mentioned what a beautiful woman you are. Tate has a gorgeous friend."

On instinct, my eyes roll, and I look him in the face. "What the fuck do you want? If you're going to kill me, please get it over with. You woke me up in the middle of the fucking night and I'm exhausted." I arch my brows at him and continue. "This could've been done during the day time."

Asher stares at me for what seems like hours, then he throws his head back and laughs. *Yeah, very fucking funny I think to myself.*

"God, there's something about you. I just can't figure out what it is." He starts to trail his fingers down my arm again, but this time I jump up and walk over by the window. I can hear the bastard chuckling.

Maybe I'll see someone outside and I can summon help. The only people outside are a bunch more of his guys, dressed exactly the same.

I look back at him, I'm more worried, not about myself, but about my friend. I've heard so many horrible things about the Mancini's, shit, I've seen bad things.

From disrespect to other small things, members can be killed for no reason.

"Are you going to hurt her?" My voice is soft but loud enough for him to hear.

Asher sighs as he walks towards me. He presses his body against my back like he can't get close enough. "I'm not personally going to, but she's going to have to pay for what she's done."

My eyes fill up with tears. I don't want him to see me cry. I don't want to be around this anymore, this isn't a family, this is a fucking business transaction. He's standing too close to me, which is doing things to my body that I don't want, especially from this type of man.

"Leave," I snap out. I just hope he's listening and does as I ask.

He wraps his arms around me, his arms barely brush against my nipples causing them to harden. "There's something about you that I find irresistible."

He looks over at his men and nods. The two shadows I saw earlier plus one more guy silently make their way out. Awesome, I'm going to have to check every inch of Tate's house before I can go back to sleep.

"Go out with me," he never moved from his position, still standing right behind me.

I snort. Is this guy for fucking real? "Please leave," I say again quieter this time, maybe he'll actually get the point and leave.

Asher bends down and puts his head in the crevice of my neck and inhales deeply. "I'll see you around, Avery." I can hear the threat in his words, Asher Mancini is not done with me, not by a long shot.

Shivers take over my whole body. The kind where you are just so fucking cold, and it won't go away. It's not that I'm turned on by him, I mean he is hot. It's his undeniable power that exudes from his pores. I bet women drop at his feet constantly.

When the door clicks, I finally breathe a sigh of relief and exhale the breath I've been holding, which makes my dumb ass cough. Damn, he fucked up my body and my head in that short time being here.

I quickly run over to Tate's side of the bed just to make sure my friend is okay. She's sound asleep, slightly snoring. She never knew her uncle was in here, at least he left her alone.

I glance at the clock and it's two-thirty in the morning. I crawl back in bed with an extra comforter just to get rid of the chill and the shivers. I know I'm not going back to sleep for a while. I left my light on after I searched the house, but it's dead silent and I don't feel anybody in here anymore.

Now, I've got to figure out how the hell we're going to get him to let Tate finish up her senior year of high school.

I have no freaking clue how we're going to accomplish this. It's not like I can ask the crime lord for an extension. I can see Asher laughing in our face.

Maybe I could find something on him that we could use. I laugh a little too loudly at that. Yes, let's try to blackmail a man who kills people for a living, that should work.

Fuck, I'm not exactly sure what to do, but I know this will break Tate's heart if she's pulled out of school.

I doubt if I'm going to find anything I can use against them, but maybe I can learn more about the family.

At first, I was going to reach for my phone, but this is the work for a laptop.

MY STOMACH IS UNSETTLED, AND I FEEL LIKE I'M GOING TO get sick from the multiple pages that I've been searching. The violence created for and by the Mancini's is horrible. No wonder Tate ran away.

I glance around the extravagant house one more time and realize I've never met her parents or an adult that is watching over her. How in the hell did Tate land herself this house? I seriously doubt it's a Mancini house, you can't really hide if you are in one of your family's multiple homes. She has someone helping her, but who?

Her brother's look just like her with dark hair, but different colored eyes, ranging from dark blue to light blue. Her oldest brother looks downright mean and unforgiving. I know that Tate was telling me about how they'll beat her, but one of them is nice. I imagine that's the one smiling with his arm wrapped around her.

I've been around these people before. I have to find their weakness and just work on that, or just keep Asher occupied with excuses until Tate graduates.

A plan starts to form in my head as I smile. I want to wake up Tate right now, but I'll let her sleep. Tomorrow we've got a lot of work to do and a lot of begging.

It never hurts anyone to beg, especially if it's for the greater good. Not for selfish reasons, like you've already had three slices of pie and you want the last one, but your mother who slaved over baking hasn't had a slice yet.

I feel more relaxed now and more invested in my day tomorrow. I'm tired but not as much as I was earlier. I still need a few more hours of sleep.

My head won't shut up, telling me to go and wake her up so we can spend the next three hours planning. The actual action will only require a few minutes of work.

I know. Tate's not going to be happy with my idea, but it's better than nothing. It's better to get that out of the way. Who knows, maybe her brothers will be happy to see her, to know she's okay. But I know none of this is true. I've been around my share of these men, they don't relent unless it's in their best interest.

For the first time in a long time, I fall asleep with a smile on my face. I love solving problems, I just hope this works.

CHAPTER 5

Asher

"Fuck," I growl as I jump up from my bed, another sleepless night. Ever since I've come face-to-face with Avery Stone, I haven't been able to do anything else except think of her.

I walk my naked ass to my en suite bathroom and start to stroke the fuck out of the prick that has his mind only on one thing, *her*.

I have never felt this way about another woman before, even women I've been with for long periods of time, more than a night and less than a week. Avery invades every single thought that I have, every breath, every second she is right there. She won't fucking go away.

I shiver as my release splashes against the cold tile in the shower. The bastard just keeps coming and coming like he's never released in his life before. All I can see is her face, eyes, and every curve of her delectable body. I've never seen her bare skin. I've absolutely no fucking clue what she looks like naked.

I want to say maybe I'm just crushing like a high schooler. This isn't crushing, this is a fucking obsession. I always get what I want, what I need. I'll make sure that somehow, someway, she becomes mine.

As I get dressed, I ignore the ringing of my cell phone. It happens to be the biggest pain in my ass, Armani. My nephews have a weird fixation on their sister, not in a sexual way, but in the way that they demand her respect. They want her to fall in line with how all the other Mancini women are.

The bastard's been calling me non-stop since I've been back for the past couple days. He's five years older than me, but it doesn't mean shit. I'm still the head of the family and he needs to abide by my rules.

I walk down to the kitchen. The walk takes at least five minutes in this fucking mansion that the Mancini's have had for generations. This isn't a mansion, it's a damn compound.

In my house, I'm not going to be dressed in a suit all the time. I'm going to relax and be fucking comfortable, even though I don't let my guys who are on duty be that way. A lot of them smile and smirk at me as I walk by.

That's fine, but they know better never to say anything. I'll end them, as I've ended others for being disrespectful. There's only a few people in this world that can say exactly how they feel, tell me when I'm being a fucking dumbass and get away with it. These guards are definitely not it.

I work my way into the kitchen just in a pair of joggers. When I was younger, I used to hate to walk with bare feet on any flooring in this house. My parents never cared enough about the house. It was just a place to sleep and eat. We only had a part-time maid, she was able to keep up with the basics of house cleaning. Flooring and other things were always overlooked. Maybe I have a foot fetish, I can't stand anything touching my feet. As much as I pay everybody, they better make sure that my damn house is spotless.

Nobody steals from me, not saying that it's never happened before, it has, and they've all paid for it. That's why we pay more than any other family to our servants, just to keep everybody in line.

Plus, they also know what would happen to them if they were to get out of line. This includes guards, maids, any services, even our acquaintances.

We didn't get this big letting everybody walk all over us. Our ancestors didn't come over from Italy for nothing. They worked their asses off to build a new life for us.

We're not in the most legal of businesses, actually we've got our hands in a bunch of shit we shouldn't have, but if it wasn't us then somebody else would be doing it. At least this way I can control more of it. The only thing I won't go into is the sex trade, because of our thoughts on women and children.

I cringe as I open the fridge thinking of Tate's older brother's, they've been trying to get me to do this for a long time. Yeah, it will double our income. I haven't done things that I'm proud of, but I don't even know if I can handle living with that on my conscience. Some women deserve to be put there, but there is a lot that are innocent, and they don't.

I grab the whole milk jug from the fridge and start chugging it. I've always done this since I was a kid. Milk is the one thing that I love to drink, I cannot live without it. There are four gallons in the fridge just waiting for me.

I hear laughing behind me, causing me to quickly turn around. I know I'm sporting a milk mustache, but I still will cut a fucker.

I laugh when I notice that it's Doppler, one of the few that can give me shit.

I made the mistake of confiding in him. "So, that girl kept you up most the night, huh?" He laughs as he comes over and grabs the jug out of my hand and pours himself a glass.

Doppler was never a really huge drinker of milk before he came to work for me. This is something that's always readily available around here. Yeah, there's water and soda and other shit, but thankfully everybody prefers this. Nobody has dared yet, besides those close to me, to make fun of me. I would get jokes all the time, like if I want cookies to dip in the milk or if I need it warm so I can go to sleep, *fuckers*.

"Piss off," I growl at him as he laughs and heads over to the island to sit down.

"You are the fucking boss, the fucking king, and you're sitting here obsessing over a girl. Just go grab her and fuck her out of your system, get it over with."

"That's not exactly the problem I'm having. I have never obsessed over a girl before." When I'm in the mood I just grab what I want to fuck.

41

My phone rings from the pocket in my joggers making me growl. On instinct I know exactly who's calling. I don't even need to look. It won't stop ringing.

I smile realizing what I'm going to do. A more humane approach of what I'm going to do. If it doesn't work, then I'll just take what I want.

"Armani," I snap out as I answer the phone. He knows I like him as much as he likes me. There's nothing more in this world he would like better than if I died, because he's the next one in line. He also knows what I'll do to him if he tries anything. I won't show any mercy at all for that kind of shit.

"So, did you find her? We've been waiting to hear from you."

"Yes, I did find her," I say nonchalantly, not giving out any more information just to fuck with him.

"Where's the bitch at? Is she back?" He growls out, his patience running thin.

I know that if she was here with me, they would end their meeting and come home right away. The brothers are in Chicago dealing with one of our contacts that's been fucking up. By dealing with, I mean getting rid of him and finding us a new contact.

As mad as they are, I doubt she would even stand a chance, they'd probably kill her. Punishment will need to be served, but I want to be able to control it. My niece does need to repent, but she doesn't deserve to die.

"No, she's not here yet, and she won't be here for a while. There's some business that I need to handle first."

"Where the fuck is she? We'll go get her our damn selves," Armani whisper yells at me. He is pushing me.

"No, you won't, she is part of the business that I need to handle." There's no way in hell I'll tell him I need to use his sister so I can get closer to Avery.

If nothing else works, I'm just going to take the damn girl. I decided this a few minutes ago, my body relaxes, and the stress seems to have left since I made this decision. The only problem with that is if I claim her as mine, then she'll become a target. All the miserable assholes I've pissed off in the past and the future will go after her, so I need to play this right.

I need to get Avery out of my head, then I won't think of her anymore. I've got to play my cards right. I have never claimed a woman, even the ones that I have gone out with. I just use them, then send them on their way.

"How can Tate possibly help you with anything?" My fuckhead of a nephew hisses at me.

"It's none of your fucking business. You'll wait until I bring her home, then you can have your redemption under my watchful eye. You need to quit fucking questioning my judgment and do what you're supposed to." I'm practically growling at him.

"Got it boss," he snaps out. I know he's got more shit he wants to say. I should have talked to my other nephew Gino, he's the nicest. This doesn't mean he's a big teddy bear, he'll kill and beat the shit out of others for no reason. He still is very deadly.

Tate and Gino have a really good relationship, but Armani will go after him if he doesn't stick to the code. Gino will still do everything he can to protect his sister. I imagine when she gets home a massive family fight will break out, and I'll be there to stop it. The other brother,

Rocco, is not as bad, but right up there with Armani. In this business nobody's going to bow down for nice people.

I hang up the phone, it's another little quirk that I have with my guys, never hang up on me, I always hang up first. It's more of a power trip than anything else. It forces them to respect me, even when they're being dicks. If anyone were to hang up on me, I'll stop whatever I'm doing to find and beat the shit out of them.

I'm not a saint, I've hit and taught a lesson to women, only those that deserve it, like beating the shit out their kids or the elderly. I've never hit a child though and I don't plan to start that any time soon.

I cringe when I think about if Armani was in charge. There would be no order, everything would be pure chaos. The Mancini's would have their toes dipped in every pool.

Head of the family was passed down to me from my father. Even if my nephews' father was in charge, it still would've been passed to me. I enjoy watching how crazy being passed up makes Armani, but there is nothing he can do about it.

I turn around and look over to Doppler who's got a huge grin on his Asian face. "What's the plan, boss?"

We both know what he's talking about, and he's definitely not talking about Tate or any other Mancini's, he's talking about Avery. I haven't decided yet.

"I don't know man," I say as I shake my head. I haven't been this nervous and excited about something before. Damn, a fucking woman is making me feel this way.

Doppler full out laughs, an explosive laugh. It takes

him a full minute to calm down. "We should probably figure something out."

I wanted to leave last night, right after the meeting, but I was hoping to sleep. "Get us ready to go back to California." If she doesn't let me court her, then I'll just take her. I'm fairly certain everything will be in my favor, since I'm letting her best friend finish up senior year.

I skipped my senior year in New York for work, I'm gonna finish it up with friends, family, and the girl I've been obsessing over. I don't have any reason or need to graduate, but now I do. Having a diploma never hurts, it doesn't help in my line of work, but who knows, one day maybe I'll do my own thing. I laugh inside my head, yeah right, I am built for being the head of the east coast, and now maybe the west coast.

He smiles at me even after I'm done talking and thinking. "Fuck you dude," I laugh.

We know that this woman is not going to volunteer to go with a Mancini, especially the way she looked at us as we were going down the stairs. That's the image of her I just can't get out of my head.

I've seen her in pictures since I've been back. Fuck, I probably know more about her than her family does.

Avery's body was fucking perfect. She's definitely a lot shorter than I am, but the right size. I imagine I got a good half a foot on her. Her eyes, they just suck you in with their innocence. Her body is perfect with delectable curves.

Fuck, my dick is starting to get hard again. I remain seated; that's all I need is Doppler to give me shit for that now, too.

After a few minutes I stand up, getting ready to make my way back to the room, and look at Doppler. "I want to leave in the next couple of hours. Make sure the plane is ready, pack what we need, we'll be gone for a year. Rent us a decent place to stay, not a dirty ass shithole." Doppler groans realizing what my plan is. "Actually, on second thought, I think we'll stay with Tate."

"Got it boss," I hear him say as I walk away followed by his laughter that echoes throughout the house. It seems like an eternity that I'm listening to him. My happy ass needs to walk through this prison much faster.

Shit, I might actually take a nap on the airplane. This is the most relaxed I've felt in the past several days, since we've been back, and it's all because of one woman.

I'll see you soon Avery.

CHAPTER 6

AVERY

I fist pump the air and dance around as I finally find the missing shoes that we seem to lose constantly.

I'm blasting classical rock, high enough to where the neighbors won't complain, but not too low. Between Arya and Garret, I'm definitely the clean freak. Thankfully, they are away working, so I'm able to clean without being bothered or asked if I'm okay since I'm cleaning.

I hear a hiss that's loud enough to overtake the music as I look over to Garett's La-Z-Boy recliner.

I hiss back at the little fucker sitting there. Sneaker is an asshole that the Stones have had forever. The white gray Persian cat gives me a dirty look, then he goes to lick his paw as he cleans himself. Everybody that would visit would end up being out one less shoe, all the damn time. The ones that he liked more, they would lose their shoes more often.

I quickly grab the five single shoes in my arms and go put two of them that are Arya's in her room. I return the other three that are mine, I'm happier that I have my sandals back. They're not overly expensive, but for me these were a rare find, plus they're comfortable as fuck.

I spend the next hour cleaning, as Sneaker just sits on the La-Z-Boy and shows me his endless disapproval. It's not that I think he doesn't like me, I believe it's his resting bitch face, which makes him absolutely adorable.

Arya and Garret Stone are what I would call silent partners with the family. There was no denying or even arguing when my grandfather called them, looking for a safe place for me to go. They still get most of the benefits of being a Romano, they only need to act when called upon, which is rare.

I like living here with them and I get along great with Arya. Mostly we just tell each other stories from the past. Arya misses my mom almost as much as I do. They were close when they were younger.

They don't treat me like a child, more like an equal. To be honest, I know those two saved me. After everything I experienced, they did whatever they could to help me. I will forever be grateful.

The Stone's live modestly, nothing like the rest of the Romano's. The house is a typical two-story home with five bedrooms and three bathrooms. It doesn't take thirty minutes to find one of them if I have a question, like it did at home. This house is comfortable. I feel like I am safe and at home. One of the houses down the street went up for sale when I first got here and it sold for almost three-million dollars, so we definitely aren't slumming it. I love how they don't need to advertise their wealth, like the rest of the family.

I know they have money, lots of it. Garrett is an extremely successful investment banker, plus I'm sure Arya receives something from the family. Unless you've been ousted, the Romano's will always take care of each other.

There were always people in and out at our house, plus my father would be gone most nights. I'm fairly certain my parents were not a silent part of the family. I sigh wishing I wasn't in such shock that I would've asked my grandfather why my mom said he was dead.

I know Arya and Garrett are concerned about me, and it's not just a family thing. They actually care about my emotional and physical well-being. I just wish they were here more. I've seen them maybe three times since I moved here.

They come home and rest and get their stuff ready for the next trip. I'm asked at least twenty times if I'm okay before they leave, *I'm not.* Usually I have to push them out the door the next day. They've never been around teenagers, even though I'm remarkably close to being an adult.

The loneliness is the worst, I'm just grateful I have Tate. Maybe one day I'll be able to grow closer to the Stone's, well, if they ever stayed longer than one night.

Next time they come home I'm gonna have to get resourceful and convince them to stay longer. I have a shit ton of questions that need to be answered before I start looking for the truth myself. *Why did my mom pretend she didn't know my grandfather? Why did I never know about them?* Plus, a bunch more, but those two are the most important.

I shake my head on the way to my shower, I stink. Right before I decide to jump in, my phone rings. I sigh before walking over there. My ass is sweaty from cleaning for so long, and my shirt is stuck to my back and my chest. Ugh, I really need a shower.

"Hello," I answer, praying that it's a fast phone call.

"Avery," Tate whispers. This causes the hairs on the back of my neck to stand up. This is the same way she acted before when she begged me not to come over to her house.

"Oh no, what's wrong?" I have a feeling that I'm not going to take a shower.

"You need to get out now," she doesn't whisper this time. "I'm leaving, I can't stick around waiting. If Asher doesn't know that I'm on the run he will very soon, and I can guarantee the next place he'll look is your house."

Fuck, I really want to shower. "Maybe you could've told me this a while ago?"

"I've been trying to call your dumb ass for hours," she snaps back at me.

"Cleaning day," I mumble out.

"Now I see. Either way babe, you need to leave now. Don't mess with the Mancini's. Please leave."

I growl out and I snap, "fine. I'll give you a call or send you a text message when I'm safe."

Tate releases the breath she must've been holding. "Good and don't take long. I love you." After she says the last part, she hangs up the phone.

I stare at the shower longingly, but wherever I end up, which most likely will be a cheap hotel or something, I can take a shower there. I need to get my ass in gear. I need to leave and get to a safe place until I can have Arya contact my grandfather.

The first thing I do, because I'm afraid that I'll forget, is to seek out two extra bowls and fill them with food and water for Sneaker. I'll make sure that he's safe even if I have to get someone to come and grab him, this will buy us at least three or four days until Arya and Garrett return. If he was a normal cat it would buy at least a week or two, but he's a little shit that eats his weight in food every day.

He just looks at me weird as I run around the place. I quickly run over to Sneaker and give him a kiss on his wrinkled nose, making him take a swat at me. He seems like an ass, but I know he loves it.

I head to my room next. Tate's uncle seems pretty obsessed with her whereabouts and what goes on with her life. I'm also certain that he's on his way to get her and I sure as shit don't want to be around.

Arya and Garrett were always scared what could happen even in the event of emergency, home intruders, robberies, the Romano way of life, etc., so we've been practicing what they refer to as a bug out bag.

It has essential shit I would need if there was a dire emergency and I didn't have time to pack everything. I'm thinking right now is one of those emergencies. I say a little silent 'thank you.'

The bag has three-thousand and sixty dollars that I've been able to save. Arya and Garrett suggested that we had ten grand. Money will always get you out of sticky situations.

I also put a few days' worth of clothes in. Of course,

they're leggings and just T-shirts, which hardly takes up any room, but they're clean and they're close.

I've also got a small first-aid kit that I designed myself with just some aspirin, ibuprofen, a bunch of Band-Aids, toothpaste, toothbrush, brush, and a box of tampons. There is no makeup at all inside my bag.

I know I don't have to stay hidden, it's Tate they're looking for, but I do want to be a little bit incognito right now. I definitely want to stay unnoticeable. I don't doubt for a second the Mancini's would use me to get to Tate, that's what my family would do.

There are some places that rent apartments in cash and if paid in advance they won't put your name on the lease agreement. These places are usually shitholes, but it's either that or a crappy hotel room, both options honestly suck.

For some reason I have to double and triple check everything. It feels like I'm forgetting something. What if a fire starts, or maybe Sneaker doesn't have enough food and water. I shake my head and take a deep breath. I've got everything I need, I'm going to do one last pass, look through the place and I'm out of here.

But first, I think to myself as I go to our bathroom and grab my favorite perfume. What can I say, the shit's expensive.

Even though he can be a shithead, my heart hurts leaving him. I go over to Sneaker and rub him on the head, he decides to purr making my heart swell. I give the little bastard a kiss on top of the head. "Be good you little shit, your owners should be home soon." He just glares at me.

Okay, I can't put off the inevitable any longer. I need to get this over with. Besides, on a brighter note, it may not be as bad as we think, and we can always come back. Yeah right, I shake my head as I put on my jacket and swing my backpack over my shoulder. Just being in Asher's presence was hard. I seriously doubt we're coming back. Hopefully, Tate and I can stay with my grandfather for a while, wishful thinking.

There's a deadbolt and a regular lock keeping us safe. Whenever we go somewhere we never lock the deadbolt, we'd always prefer to get in faster. My aunt could have guards stationed everywhere if she felt like it, courtesy of the Romano's. She won't, which is one of the things I love about her, everything is so much more simpler here, more comfortable.

I lock the bottom lock after I open the door. That's enough in case Tate does come by.

I promised myself I wouldn't turn around and take one more last longing look at the place I shared for the last several months with my new family. *I failed miserably.*

I quickly wipe away the tears as I realize this might be the last time I see them for a while.

"Screw it," I growl out as I quickly swing back towards the open door. I don't know if I mistook how much I swung around but I end up going face first into a brick wall. This brick wall is softer than the new siding on the house that was recently installed.

"Easy there," the deep voice penetrates through my skin, chilling me everywhere. I slowly risk glancing up awkwardly. My breath catches as I look into the bright blue eyes of Asher Mancini.

"Sorry. I didn't realize anybody was there." I stammer as I try to quickly compose myself. I take a step back putting much needed space in between us.

I look back and glare at Sneaker. Bastard, the door is open, he should be trying to run out like he always does. At least I would have a reason to leave, to chase him. My backpack's not big enough to where it looks like I'm actually going on a holiday, but more like I've got a shit ton of homework.

I make sure not to maintain eye contact, as Asher continues to breathe deeper. *Relax* I scold myself, just because he's here, doesn't mean anything. I've still got a chance. If I play this right, both Tate and I will be fine, safe.

Asher doesn't move, he continues to block the door. Several of his men are standing right behind him. I recognize the biggest one as the guy who was here the other day, he seems really close to Asher. *Oh God*, I'm in deep shit.

Asher holds out his hand in a waving motion letting me know that he wants to go back in the apartment. *I can get out of this, right?*

Show no fear, Avery, show no fear.

CHAPTER 7

ASHER

I laugh as my latest obsession, I should say my only obsession, runs right smack into me. All I want to do is reach out my hand to grab onto her and keep her close to me, but now is not the time.

She awkwardly apologizes before she even looks up and realizes who I am, but the moment she does is when the expression on her face morphs into something totally different. Mainly I see shock, but I can also see what looks like fear. Disappointment flares up inside as I realize she's scared, not a trace of excitement in my presence.

I give her a nod not moving. I can tell she was on her way out the door, but this is my perfect opportunity to talk to her. I motion for her to go back inside as her head drops in defeat. She turns around and drops herself right at the edge of their couch.

She looks longingly at the La-Z-Boy recliner they have, but some furball is taking residence on it. Maybe she figured this was the only way to get away from me.

Doppler gives me a look of concern, he knows what I'm thinking. Liam gives me a look of confusion. I don't talk as much to Liam as I do Doppler. Doppler knows the strange fascination, fuck that, obscene obsession that I have with this girl in front of me.

I walk as slow as I can, she never takes her eyes off of me, which is good. When she's scared, this'll make things that much more fun.

Doppler softly closes the door behind him when he walks in. I know that Devon and Liam will remain outside to keep a lookout even though they don't need to. I've got a shit ton of my men here. With as many threats against my life on a daily basis, I keep a lot of backup.

I close the distance between us and make sure to sit right next to her, even though there's a whole couch available. I'm not missing this opportunity to be as close to her as I can.

As soon as I sit down, Avery jumps up in a panic and looks between me and Doppler and asks. "Do you guys want something to drink?"

She doesn't wait for us to tell her anything as she hurries straight towards the kitchen. Doppler presses his lips together, I know he's doing whatever he can to keep from laughing. I should kick the fucker outside but he's staying in here for my benefit and for hers.

I've never felt this way about a girl, and I have no idea what my obsession will drive me to do. It's better that there's somebody in here with us, mainly to protect her from me.

No matter what, I'll have her one way or another, but having a compliant woman is easier on me, and more enjoyable than having a woman that I have to fight all the time. Don't get me wrong, a good fight is always fine, especially when I know I'll win in the end. Since this is just the beginning, I need to be careful.

Avery stumbles back to the living room before she regains her composure. I can see the moment a mask slips over her beautiful bright features. My girl looks comfortable today, like she's just going to do errands.

In her hands she's got several bottles of water, it looks like she grabbed one for Devon and Liam, that's nice.

She comes and sits down on the other side of the couch after she hands us our drinks. Her head is down as Doppler looks to me and smiles and shakes his head. He knows that I need to be next to her, even though I probably should give her some space, but fuck it.

After she sat down, I get up moving myself closer to her.

I lean closer to her letting my arm press against hers as my head leans down to the crook of her neck. "Where are you from Avery?"

She snaps her head in my direction and says, "Oh, um, I'm from Chicago. I'm just here to finish my senior year." She glances nervously between Doppler and me. "Only my senior year to go, yay."

"What do you plan on doing after you graduate?" I ask leaning back, making myself more comfortable.

I should be taking care of business, but I'm fascinated by this creature sitting next to me. I'm going to use every advantage I have to get her under me and find out more about her. Not the kind of shit that I can look up online, I want to know what she'll tell me face-to-face.

"I haven't decided yet." Looks like she's starting to relax, she must really be proud of her schooling and her education. "I imagine I'm just going to get a job or go to college somewhere."

Darkness passes through her eyes as she said last part. If I didn't know any better I would say she was hiding from someone or something. I know it couldn't be me, because she has no reason to fear me yet, stupid girl.

I know I shouldn't, but my body has a mind of its own as I inch my way closer to her again. I just can't get enough of her. Even though she's sitting to my left, my whole body is angled that way.

I'd bend her over the back of the couch right now, give us what we both deserve and then go grab my niece and get the fuck out of here. I won't have to worry about this girl anymore and this hold she has on me.

My hands turn into fists, but I quickly will them away not wanting her to see that there's anger flowing in me. It's not her fault but I definitely don't like this power that she has over me. This is where lives can be lost, shit can go downhill really fast.

The Mancini's and other families of the East Coast are reliant on me, so another horrible family doesn't step up and take over. I'm not on my game and I'm not playing to the best of my abilities. If this girl is keeping me down I gotta do something about it.

There's nothing more I want to do except keep myself where I'm at, at the top. I worked too long and too fucking hard for one woman to bring down the whole empire. I'll do everything I can first before taking her with me or send her away.

Avery got the short end of the stick. I should feel bad, but all it does is gravitate me closer to her, I just want to be near her.

Her scent is intoxicating. A mixture of coconut vanilla and what must be pure Avery, her natural musk. I lean a little closer and take a huge breath, this act alone gives me the shivers. It feels fucking fantastic being this close to her.

I glance over to Doppler who is watching us with a stern expression. "Get out," I snap at him.

He gives me a look of concern and I crease my eyebrows in warning. We might be close, but nobody will fucking get in my way when I want something. Doppler gives me a nod, then heads out the front door.

I can hear Avery take in a gasp of breath as she stares between the door and me. Maybe for some subconscious reason she felt a little bit comfortable with somebody else in the room with us, but that's gonna change.

I want her without any distractions between us. I know I should calm myself down or allow reasoning to seep through my hardened brain, but I honestly don't give a fuck.

I always get what I want.

Avery quickly jumps up knowing that something's about to happen, she's going on instinct. I grab her waist and place her back down in my lap. She's so busy trying to get back up not paying attention, I'm able to easily spin her around until she's straddling me.

The girl practically weighs nothing. I use one of my hands to pin both of hers behind her back. The moment makes me groan as her chest flares out more to my face.

"What are you doing?" She whispers, her face full of fear.

My free hand goes down to her hip as I push her harder into my lap letting her know exactly how much I want her. Her nipples turn into hard little buds through the stretched thin T-shirt she's wearing. That makes me groan more, tilting my head back a little bit. Her mind might not want me, but her body disagrees.

My hand leaves her hip and travels up, lightly skimming the side of her. "For some strange reason I can't get you out of my head, out of my thoughts," I tell her as my finger flicks back and forth over her nipple.

Avery slightly moans and quickly tries to cover it up, but it's too late, I heard it. And if that doesn't make my dick harder, I don't know what will.

I lean my head down to the crook of her neck and inhale deeply, her scent is both intoxicating and intriguing. It's like she was made for only me.

I don't even know what I'm thinking anymore, the only thing I can concentrate on is this girl in my lap.

I feather light kisses along her neck and on the sides of her mouth. My free hand is grabbing her by the back of her head, yanking her back, so I have access to everything I want.

My dick is so hard it's straining against my pants wanting to come out. I know she can feel it because I keep reminding her every time she moves, I am able to perfectly hit hard against her center core. I bet my left nut's fucking blue as hell.

I glance around the room hoping to find anything that will allow me to restrain her hands. I would love to be able to use both mine to play, but there's nothing in sight. This place is immaculately clean and clutter free.

I groan, but I remind myself I still have one hand. It eagerly has a mind of its own, dirty bastard, as it travels down and presses against her core. It only takes me two seconds to find her sweet spot. Her legs are pushed open from straddling mine.

Avery moans, despite fighting and doing everything she can to keep the sound from reaching out to me. It was unmistakable and I definitely heard it.

A loud thump knocks me out of my stupor as I pull her tightly against my body, then look around the room. That's when I notice a backpack that she uses for school, it must have fallen.

I see some of the contents as they spill out. This wouldn't bother me, but the part that does bother me is a toothbrush and toothpaste that happened to roll out of the top, because it wasn't closed all the way.

I lift her off of me and set her on the couch with her leg touching mine. "Don't move," I snap as a grab the backpack off the ground and open it.

She sees what I'm doing as a gasp escapes her. She tries to reach her hand out to grab the bag from me, but I smack it away. "Don't fucking move, or I'll tie you down." I'm lying, but she doesn't need to know that. My words do what they were intended to, and she backs down.

Avery is shaking and she's so pissed, her jaw is clenched so hard that I'm afraid she might actually crack a couple teeth. Her hands are fisted in her lap, she's a fighter.

I start searching the bag and find an envelope of cash,

plus a bunch of clothes and other personal items. The shit in this bag is for someone intended on leaving, not for school. Even though school doesn't start for several more days.

I put back everything in the bag and zip it up properly. I casually lean back against the couch and look over at her. "Where are you going Avery?"

She shakes her head and replies, "nowhere."

"Yeah right," I snarl. I don't see how she can lie herself out of this one.

The moment has passed. It doesn't take much to get me turned on by this girl, but right now I've got another pressing matter.

My hand quickly shoots out as it wraps around her throat. "Where is Tate?" I growl out. To her it probably sounds like a hiss.

She takes in a deep breath and I know that I got my point across. This girl is scared, and it looks like she's on the fucking run.

"Fuck," I snap out as I shoot off the couch. I turn around and glare at her. "Don't you fucking move."

Her mouth is open now, she's taking deep breaths. She should be afraid right now, very fucking afraid. My body starts to tremble again, but it's not in excitement for her, it's in anger.

These two fucking girls tried to pull a fast one on me, they almost got away with it. I imagine if I was five minutes later, shit, probably even one minute later, she would've been gone.

I look towards the door and snap out, "Doppler, Devon." Knowing my guys will come right in, which they do, leaving Liam to stand guard.

Guns are drawn, they must've heard the anger, and the fear, and the disappointment in my voice.

"Boss," Doppler says as he looks around, his eyes landing on a very terrified and pissed off Avery.

"Tate's made a run for it, we need to find her now." I growl out, both Devon and Doppler don't look surprised. They know how much my niece hates her family. That she'll do anything that she can to stay away.

"Doppler, stay here with her. Make sure she doesn't go anywhere or do anything stupid."

I relax my pace as I stomp back over to an exceedingly small and intimidated looking Avery. I've seen people scared and this just doesn't look real, like she's trying to be more scared than she actually is.

I bend down and wrap my hand around her throat yanking her up to a standing position. "Where the fuck is she?" Her face starts to turn red fast, I know I'm cutting off her circulation.

She gasps out, "I don't know. I just want to leave."

With my other hand I pat down her pants knowing that there's not a place for a cell phone in her leggings. I've seen most girls just put them in the elastic band. I find her phone and I quickly throw it over to Devon so that he could start looking through it.

Time is wasting for me to get information out of her. I want her, we have too much of a connection, well my dick has more of a connection with her.

I release her neck and she instantly plops back down on the couch, she covers herself with both of her arms.

"Don't you fucking move, do you understand me?" Avery nods still gasping for the precious air that she lost.

I don't look back as Devon and I head out the door.

This whole situation blows, this is something that I don't have time for right now. I curse myself, she was right at my fingertips. If I wasn't so enamored by her friend, I would have Tate and we'd be back in fucking New York already. Yeah right, I can't leave this girl yet.

Now I have to search through a state I don't know that much about trying to find my fucking niece, but at least I have help.

I'm gonna have to hold on to Avery for a while. I know she's irritated that her best friend put her in this predicament. It won't be long till my niece willingly comes crawling back to me.

In the meantime, maybe I'll be able to fuck this girl out of my system or at least have a little bit of fun.

Devon sees the smile on my face, and he breaks out in uncontrollable laughter. "You are so fucked up," he manages to choke out through his laughter.

My tension quickly snaps to him and I know he can see the anger and resentment on my face as he quickly snaps his mouth shut.

Right now, I'm in between wanting to find her and not wanting to find her. I laugh to myself as Devon gets in the driver's seat and pulls us away. Even if I find Tate, it doesn't matter, I'm still going to fuck her friend, hopefully when I get back.

If Avery only knew what she was getting herself into.

CHAPTER 8

Avery

I watch as the huge tank makes his way into the room and plants himself right in the recliner. Sneaker doesn't do anything, he just looks at him. The little bastard didn't even try to help.

Whenever the doors would open, he'd always try to run out to get us to chase him, but now that we have dangerous company, he seems fine. Maybe if he realized that these guys could take away his precious food and also Tate, he loves Tate, then he would actually try to help us.

I giggle inwardly as I imagine Sneaker jumping on Doppler's face, scratching him over and over again. The big guy runs out of the apartment screaming like a girl as he has a cat attached to his face.

We sit in silence for five minutes until Sneaker gets up and starts to rub against the enemy.

My guard absentmindedly scratches Sneaker on his head. Great, there's so much I wish I could be doing, besides sitting here and watching our traitorous cat.

Fuck, why didn't I just leave a few minutes earlier? If I did that there'd be no problems whatsoever. These guys don't strike me as the type to hurt a defenseless traitorous animal for no reason, so Sneaker should be fine. I glance over in their direction, obviously the little shit's living it up.

"So, how long have you been working for the Mancini's?" I'm trying to do whatever I can to pass the time or maybe get a good rapport with this guy so I can sneak out.

He turns his attention towards me, his eyes narrow slits. "Long enough," he states, letting me know that that's the end of this conversation.

Awesome.

I pick my bag up off the floor and start to go through it. I seriously doubt a man like Asher Mancini would need to take four thousand dollars from me.

My money and all my belongings are still sitting in the same spot that they were. Even my box of tampons is on the top. My younger self would've been mortified by him seeing this, but my older self doesn't give a shit. There's more important things to be worried about now. Like how can I get myself out of this situation. I remember my phone but then I also remember that it's currently sitting in Doppler's hands.

But seeing the tampons gives me an idea. "Can I use the restroom?" A minute has passed, and he still doesn't respond to me. "Or I could just pee right here." I can see a shiver of disgust go through him.

"Two minutes," he snaps out.

That's all I need to get away, I think to myself as I give him a pleasant smile, wrapping my bag around my shoulder. He gives me a look of concern until he remembers how high up we are and figures there's no way for me to get out.

As soon as I go to the bathroom I shut the door, leaning myself against it and closing my eyes, breathing as deeply as I can.

"God, what the hell have I gotten myself into?" I whisper to the person staring back at me in the mirror.

Two minutes, I remind myself as I jimmy open the window that's been painted shut ever since I moved in with the Stone's.

I sigh in relief as I'm able to heave the bastard open in seconds.

The only part that sucks now is that I have to jump from the second story. Luckily for me there's a thick patch of grass right at the bottom, but either way it's still going to hurt.

I throw my backpack down first. One might think it would be good for cushioning, but I actually threw it out to the side. There's still some shit in there that I don't want jabbing me in the side, like my toothbrush or even some of my other necessities I have.

I grunt as I land on my feet, leaning my body to the side so I roll. I was jumping from longer distances when I was younger, but I was smart enough to know that I don't want my legs to snap.

I stand up and wipe all the excess grass and leaves off of me. My right ankle hurts a little bit but not enough to where it's broken. I doubt if it's even sprained, I just landed on it wrong, but it could be a ton worse, I could've broken both my legs.

I glance up from where I just jumped. "Fuck," I say to myself as Doppler stares at me from the window I just vacated. I yelp in excitement as I start running for one of the spare cars the Stones have.

I stop in my tracks as I realize Asher always travels with multiple men. They're probably keeping everybody out of this area right now, the streets look empty and deserted.

"Fuck," I say as I dive behind a bush that's near the wall of the house. How the hell can I get out of here? I should just be able to walk nonchalantly to the car and drive off. *No time like the present*, I think as I straighten my shoulders and walk normally.

No one is around that I can see, but there are several black SUV's on my street that don't belong here. *Maybe they're waiting in their vehicles.*

Right, I think, hoping I'm in the clear. I lower myself into the older Audi, but I'm grabbed by the back of my head. Someone has a viselike grip as they pull my head and hair up.

I can see mischievous Doppler looking right back at me. He doesn't say anything to me as he starts to drag me back into the house.

"No, no, no," I stammer out as I try to dig my heels into the sidewalk to stop our progression. I didn't just jump from the second story window so that he can come and grab me and take me right back up there, fuck that.

He might be a huge fucking dinosaur of a tank, but I have been trained for guys that are a lot bigger than me.

He must sense what I'm about to do and I'm quickly turned upside down and thrown over his shoulder.

Before I get coherent enough to figure out my surroundings and what I was doing in the first place, the door to my house is opening and I'm being tossed on the couch.

"Dammit," I curse myself figuring I had a better chance of escaping out there, but I'm not done yet. Not even close.

Doppler turns his back towards me as I jump up, ready to attack.

He senses me right at the perfect time and whips around. I kick as hard as I can in the way I was taught, straight to the front of his kneecap. The man drops like a ton of bricks groaning out a few curse words as he looks back up to me. It's my perfect opportunity as my fist goes flying through the air and matches up perfectly with the middle of his nose.

I was always warned about hitting people here, but this guy is keeping me where I don't want to be kept. His nose explodes and a litany of curses follow right after.

I can smell the metallic scent of blood that dissipates in the air. I think it was an awesome punch, I shattered this mother-fucker's nose.

As much as I would love to stick around and watch him as he holds his nose together, I don't. I grab my backpack and make a run towards the front door.

I don't even make it two steps before my ankle is harshly yanked. My body lands on the floor with a loud thump. That hurt more than jumping from the second story window. I groan out, my wrist and my kneecap hurt. I should be grateful that he didn't punch me like I just punched him.

I can hear what sounds like a belt sliding quickly out of his pants. My hands are yanked behind me and the belt securely fastens keeping me pinned down and unable to move. I'm lifted up as Doppler limps over to the couch and places me down.

"Don't move or I'll do to your nose what you just did to mine." I nod, I one hundred percent believe this guy.

I just sit, there is really not much else I can do with my hands behind my back. Escaping again does briefly cross my mind, but the front door is locked. Even if I sneak over there, that bolt is fucking loud and he'll be able to hear me from the kitchen.

I can hear him laugh from the kitchen. "Is he insane?" I ask myself. I busted his kneecap and I also shattered his nose. That shit's got to hurt, fuck, I know it hurts, it's happened to me before. Not the kneecap part, but the punch in the face has.

I shake my head as I continue to hear chuckling in there. My brain is urging me to run for the front door, leave my shit behind, just get the fuck out of here. I know that won't work. I can feel it deep down inside, he would grab me before I even have a chance to step one foot out.

I tug hard on the belt that's holding my hands, but I don't get any leeway. God, I wonder how many people he's tied up before. I shake my head, I don't even want to continue to think about that.

Okay Avery, you need to be smart. I know when I'm down and the right time to fight and right now this is not that time. I just got to plan my next move and be as careful as possible.

Doppler limps back out, before he could take a seat

next to Sneaker somebody pounds loud on the front door. He glares at me so that I don't even try anything and then whispers. "You don't want anybody else to get hurt, do you?" I snap my mouth shut.

He opens the door as Asher and Devon stroll in. I do have to admit Asher is fucking gorgeous. Even though he's been moving around and had me on his lap, his suit looks fresh. He definitely changed when he was outside.

His thighs are thick and make the material stretch around him. I know the shirt is tailored, it has to be, or that's the effect that he wanted to have. It definitely works for him.

Asher's eyes never leave mine, as he sees that my hair is a little bit out of place and my hands are behind my back. I don't say anything, I can't offer up information.

Devon starts to chuckle as Asher's eyes leave mine and they land on Doppler. If I said I wasn't nervous, I would be lying. Hell, yeah, I'm nervous, what will he do when he sees what his guy looks like?

I didn't expect him to throw his head back and howl with laughter, not at all. Doppler's eyes twinkle with mischief, messing with his boss.

"Damn girl," Devon says to me with a wink as Devon and Doppler make their way outside, shutting the door behind them.

Asher comes and sits right next to me pulling me into his lap making me wince from the bite of the leather belt digging into my skin.

"Your friend ditched you." He doesn't make it a question, just a fact. We both know the truth that Tate did

71

leave. But she didn't ditch me, she warned me, it was my fault my ass was taking too long.

I know I'm playing with fire, but I shake my head and bite my lip. "She didn't ditch me. She ditched you."

Asher smiles and he leans into me. I have a feeling that's his favorite place to be around me is with his head snuggled into my neck as he inhales deeply.

He leans back. "It looks like you're going to have to take your friend's place for a while until she comes back."

No, no, no, I shake my head. "I have nothing to do with this, this is between you and Tate. This is a family matter, I'm just here to go to school and graduate."

He looks at me with a bit of pity in his eyes, which pisses me off. I'm half tempted to head butt him, but I have a feeling I need to save everything up my sleeve so I can get away later.

"You being with me will get her back faster as soon as she realizes that you tried to get away. But don't worry if you're good I'll let you finish up your last year."

Now I'm fuming. What does he think I am, a child? "If I'm good?" I try to rearrange myself so that I can knee his balls as I get up.

Asher moves his hands underneath me, placing them right on my ass as his fingers graze close to my core. He lifts me up making me wrap my legs around him, so I don't fall backwards. He walks back down the hall knowing exactly where my room is.

Asher knows no bounds as he dumps me on my bed. For a few seconds I was nervous that he was going to follow, but luckily he reached into his pocket and pulled out what looks to be my phone.

He doesn't say anything as he crawls next to me. I'm still bound, and my hair is a freaking mess. I'm quite sure I've got all different kinds of grass and bushes in it.

He messes with my phone for a few seconds and it doesn't take long for me to figure out that he's going to take a picture of us.

A selfie with Asher, I feel like a schoolgirl.

He doesn't take a normal selfie with us sitting together, no, he lifts me up and positions me on his lap, but this time at least I'm facing forward. He makes sure the receiver will be able to see how my arms are bound and I look shitty.

Asher smiles big as he takes a snapshot. My expression is still the same, neutral, and wondering what the hell is going on.

After the picture he doesn't take me off his lap, but he does adjust me to where I'm more comfortable. He pulls up Tate's name, then starts typing.

Let's negotiate.

I'm not even sure that Tate has her cell phone anymore. I would have ditched mine, I don't want to be tracked. If she did keep it, I imagine I'm the only person to keep in contact with, since she's running away from her family.

My mouth opens wide when the call comes in less than a minute later. Asher really does know his niece.

He undoes the belt from behind me and tells me to go out to the living room. I don't move for a second, I'm frozen and happy that my restraints are gone. Plus, I also want to know what the conversation is between him and Tate.

"Tatum," he growls giving me a pointed look.

"Yeah, yeah, I got the message," I mumble to myself as I make my way out to the living area, where Doppler and Devon are just sitting there watching TV.

I instantly cringe when I see Doppler's face, he's starting to swell. "I'm sorry," I say as I sit far away from both of the men. Devon laughs as Doppler gives me a tight smile and a wink.

I shouldn't even be talking to my captors let alone trying to play nice, but for some reason I'm not really scared of these three. I've been around much worse.

I'm about to open my mouth and talk more when my bedroom door shuts and the clicking from Asher's over-priced fancy shoes on Arya's and Garrett's hardwood floor, grabs my attention.

Asher doesn't take his eyes off of me as he walks by. I'm actually glad that we're not alone right now because I don't know what he would do.

He stops in front of me tilting his head down to make sure I can look in his eyes. "I'll see you soon Avery," he growls out in annoyance as he nods towards his men.

Within the next five seconds they're out of the house and my doors are locked and I'm free.

Something must have happened with the conversation between him and Tate. For the next hour I frantically try to get ahold of my best friend, but she never picks up.

Where are you Tate?

CHAPTER 9

AVERY

"Avery, breakfast is ready!" Arya yells from the kitchen. My stomach grumbles, but for some reason I just can't stop looking in the mirror. My nerves are slowly starting to ooze from my pores.

Blackwood Academy's uniform is pretty basic and bare with their colors being brown and blue.

I've been spending the last five minutes folding the waste of my skirt and opening and closing buttons on my blouse.

I shake my head and smile, I need to just be me. I let my skirt go back to normal, which is right above my knees and button all of the buttons on my blouse except for the top one so I don't feel like I'm in a choke-hold all day.

It takes me less than a minute to get to the kitchen which is awesome. It wasn't like this at my old house, it was a long walk. I shake my head, refusing to let myself cry going back down that road again. Even if it took me a half an hour to find the kitchen, I would trade it just to see my parents again.

Arya made a huge spread of everything imaginable. I've only been with them for a few months, they know some of what I like but not everything. If I could eat more and had a better metabolism, I would grab some of everything on this table, but I know if I do that, I'll end up splitting my skirt right open, from the added weight.

I do manage to grab a lot and fill up my plate. I know I'm not going to eat it all, but I'll be eating at least half of it. I'm pretty slim for my age and I don't care what anybody thinks, I won't stop until I'm not hungry anymore. I care more about food than I do what everybody else thinks.

"Thank you, this is so good," I say as I stuff my face looking at Arya with her beaming smile.

Garrett keeps grunting and loading stuff from the house to the trunk of the car. I know they're going back on another work trip, I'm grateful that they decided to come home to help me through the first day of school.

I would be lying if I said I wasn't nervous. How could anybody not be nervous starting a new school? It sucks.

"Avery, do you need a ride?" I nod my head yes to her. I wasn't supposed to need a ride. Tate was going to pick me up and then take me home every day, but I haven't been able to get ahold of her for over a week. Dread fills my stomach as I push my plate away, *what happened to my friend?*

Did Asher Mancini do something to her? Will I ever see her again? Oh God, what if her brother got a hold of her? I feel like I'm going to get sick.

"Let's go," Garrett says with a huge grin on his face, then drops a grand on the countertop. That's the same amount of money they leave me every time they go somewhere. They come home at least once or twice a month just to stay the night and then leave again.

Most high school seniors would be ecstatic if they had this much leeway, not me. I'm really fucking lonely. But I am grateful that they're home to help me with today. Some parents don't even do that for their children, and they're not even my parents. I think they're my second cousins or some shit, grandpa just said cousins, so who knows and who cares. All that matters is they're blood.

The drive to school isn't long, maybe ten minutes. It takes longer to get up to the front entrance because everybody has to stop. The personal drivers stop in front of the school, proceed to get out and open the door for the spoiled rich kids. Every. Single. Car. Does. This, except for us.

I can tell Garrett's thinking about opening my door since he is driving but I put my hand on his shoulder as he watches me in the rearview mirror, and I shake my head no. He's not my driver or my chauffeur, he's like my uncle.

He nods and gives me a sincere smile. Arya squeezes my hand when I exit the vehicle. I realize I wanted to hug them both goodbye. I feel like crying, they're leaving me again and I'm going back to being alone.

The front of Blackwood Academy makes me gasp. It's a huge goth like compound that's all brick. Where there isn't brick, there are hundreds of windows everywhere. Gargoyles align the top of the building and stone statues of lions and various other predators lead up the walkway to the huge ten-foot double doors.

I'm getting a few sideways glances, but nobody says anything, and no one even acknowledges me. I am the new girl, as low on the totem pole as you can get, but my only concern is to find Tate and get through this day.

Thankfully, I was able to get my schedule early with help from the Stone's, no need to go to the Dean's office first thing. A few nights ago, I printed off a map of the school, then memorized as best as I could. I'm already the new girl, I definitely don't want to be the new girl that arrives late to every class so everybody can just stare at me while the teacher looks at me disapprovingly.

I can tell what clichés are what as soon as I step into the monstrosity they call the school. The hallways are long and very tall as a bunch of jocks in football uniforms run back and forth tossing the ball to each other, dodging giggling girls and everyone else. The atmosphere is happy with smiles on most kids' faces.

The popular girls look like they just got off the runway and came straight to school, they're stationed in the corner over by the jocks. They are facing they're lockers that must have mirrors, concentrating on making sure their plastic faces are pristine. I was too worried about my uniform, I forgot to even bother with makeup.

Those are the two God-like groups in this school. The stoners are in one area, while the nerds are in the other area, but it doesn't matter, everyone has their eyes on the jocks and cheerleaders, Blackwood Academy elite.

Jealousy and envy are thick in the air. Everyone

watching either wants to be them, fuck them, or they downright hate them.

I can't really say what group I'm in. I'll probably be in whatever group Tate's in, that's all that matters to me. I just pray to God it's the nerd group or something where we don't stand out.

"Watch out!" one of the guys scream causing me to turn as the football the jocks were playing with flies straight for my head. Thankfully, my reflexes are fast and I'm able to snag the thing in my arm. His eyes widen as he slows to a stop in front of me.

"Nice catch," the gorgeous God says while his eyes move up and down over me. He has the brightest blue eyes I've ever seen and is built like a linebacker. "I'm Noah," he says as he holds out his hand.

A little blush crawls up my cheeks as I hold out my hand, "I'm Avery."

I had just found my locker when the ball was launched towards my head. My body still pulses with nerves knowing he's still right next to me.

"So, you're the new girl, aren't you?"

My head snaps to him. "The new girl? Am I the only one? There are no other new kids?"

He gives me a tight smile, which somehow makes him look hotter. "You must have some pretty high-profile parents. Blackwood Academy never accepts new kids," he says while tossing the ball back to his friends. "Everyone has to start at freshman year. If you leave, you don't come back, ever. You're sort of like an enigma."

I turn around to listen to him, after he finishes the last part my head taps against the back of the locker. Great, this is going to suck knowing everyone's wondering who the hell I am and how I was able to get in.

Noah gives me a wink, then runs back over to his football mates, who all happen to be staring at me. *Awesome.*

I locate my next class easily and I start to head through the door. I'm not early but thankfully I'm not late, either.

Somebody slams into my shoulder on the side moving past me. "Watch where the fuck you're going," she snaps out. This has to be the queen of Blackwood Academy. Her minions are following her, laughing, and pointing at me as I stand there frozen, watching them find their seats.

I'm still standing there in a little bit of shock as I watch the queen bitch swing her hips towards the back. There's one seat empty, a big group of people are seated saving the middle seat for her.

There's no doubt that she's gorgeous, model gorgeous with dirty blonde hair and ocean blue eyes. This girl has money and entitlement written all over her.

I know if I don't do something about this, it's going to keep happening. I need to let this bitch know that she's going to have a fight if she keeps fucking with me. I am Mila Avery Romano, we do not stand for this shit.

I walk in, all eyes are on the new girl of course. I manage to give the English teacher and older man with a receding hairline and the start of a beer belly the brightest smile I can.

He gives me a tight smile back that reaches his eyes. Makes me feel a little sad at first knowing that everybody probably doesn't pay him any time. I'm sure the student body here treats the staff like shit, this is the land of spoiled entitlement.

I take another sip of some of the best coffee I've ever had. Garrett handed this to me as we were walking out the door. I'm not even halfway through and I really don't want to lose my coffee, but tit-for-tat and all.

I make myself look meek and scared as I pretend to walk around and look for a seat, going over in the area of the queen bitch.

They all watch as I close in on them ready for the show that's about to take place. The main girl and what looks to be her best friends, anyone knows they'll stab her in the back to move up the ladder, turn around and wait for me to get closer. They're already thinking of the things that they want to say to me. I am happy all three are sitting close together, like really close.

They had to move their chairs just so they can form their alliance and touch at the hip letting everybody know how powerful they are.

I notice the girl in front is giving me a nasty glare, her backpack is next to her on the floor. I pretend not to see it as I stumble, my coffee lid conveniently loosened when I took my last drink. I watch not withholding my grin as the coffee flies all over the three, mainly hitting the queen and her designer clothes.

Everyone is too shocked to say anything, they watch what happens. The screams and curses coming from the three girls echo down the hallway and most likely outside. I know I shouldn't have made myself a target, but there is no way in hell I will keep my head down and be afraid every minute at this new school.

I look to the teacher giving him a slight smile, that hopefully relays that I'm sorry to inconvenience him. His expression shocks me. The man has one of the brightest smiles I've ever seen on an adult. Well, I guess he really doesn't care for these assholes, either.

Returning my attention to my three new best friends, I give them my most innocent look and put my hand up to my mouth and say, "oh my gosh, I am so sorry." I purposely cringe when I look at them. "That's going to leave a bad stain and it must be so hot."

I let my face slip back into a mask of hatred as I give them a wink and head towards the front of the classroom.

Since I made it look like what I did was an accident, the main bitch keeps her voice lowered as she sneers, "you're going to pay for that you fucking cunt."

I blow them off, waving their sticky asses out of the room and take my seat, listening to all the chuckles and the pouring of laughter coming from the rest of the classroom. I guess no one has ever tried to mess with the hierarchy before.

Even though that felt good, I wince, this is going to be a long fucking day.

CHAPTER 10

Avery

Out in the hall I'm grateful I haven't run into the girls that I accidentally dumped my coffee on. The last time I locked eyes with them was right after the incident when they all got up and made sure to knock into me as they passed my seat and headed for the door. Thankfully, they never came back to class.

I don't waste a bunch of time at my locker. I keep my head down, not even paying attention to those around me as I walk into my second period trigonometry class.

I gasp as I see a solemn looking Tate in the back corner as far away as she can get from everyone.

"Oh my God." My chest feels lighter as I quickly walk in her direction. When she sees me her expression changes from sadness into one of elation.

"Where've you been?" I ask her as I pop down in the seat next to her. I really want to reach out and give her a hug. I didn't think I'd ever see her again, who knows with her fucked up family.

I don't want to embarrass or draw attention to ourselves. Honestly, I couldn't give a shit, but I'm not exactly sure how Tate feels about that.

"Family," she says as her sad smile returns.

"At least you're here." I study her for a second. "Now why in the hell couldn't you text me or let me know you were okay? You made me worry about you, shit, I was freaked out. Who knows what Asher, or your brothers, were doing to you?"

"I couldn't," she whispers as her pale blue eyes fill with tears.

'Why,' is on the tip of my tongue. I don't even have a chance to ask it when a crap ton of students start to pour into the classroom.

I give Noah a tight smile as he leads the way, followed by three other boys that are equally as hot.

My breath catches as the last boy enters followed by a ton of other classmates. Girls giggling with a hopeful chance of landing one of the hot guys, while the boys smirk like they belong.

I'm fairly certain half of these students don't even have this class. I'm proven right when a woman with black hair and stick thin limbs walks in and half of the kids run out of the classroom trying to make it to their own before the bell rings.

Asher freaking Mancini is heading towards an area in the corner of the classroom while the rest of his friends follow.

His gaze is focused on that area until his head turns, and he looks directly at me, like he knew I was there. I unintentionally summoned him.

His position changes as he walks the short distance to where me and Tate are sitting, hopeful to remain in our own little bubble. Tate notices Asher and groans, lowering herself as far as she can into her chair, most likely hoping to disappear.

The whole class freezes to watch what's happening. Asher snaps, "move," to the people in front of us. They can't get their belongings together fast enough.

Asher gives me a wink that's too overly happy, making me shiver. The gorgeous God plants himself in the row in front of me. I'm sitting against the wall and Tate is sitting to my left. I say a thankful prayer for that, that Asher didn't sit right next to me somehow.

Not much happens in the next hour as we listen to what is expected of us.

Tate and I keep texting and she gives me the run down on Asher and his group of followers. After every time she sends me a text message, she points out who she's talking about.

It would be better if we could just talk about it openly, but Miss Harris, the trigonometry teacher, keeps rambling on about how this year is going to be.

Apparently, the blonde haired, blue-eyed football player, Liam Novak is the closest to Asher Mancini. They've been friends for a long time, they just haven't been in the same school.

His family is huge. They sell everything that any baby would need, they're basically comparable to Johnson & Johnson, and I'm quite sure they're competitors.

The next one is Walker Winchester, I guess he's the only one that doesn't play football, but he likes other sports, like track. He has beautiful hazel eyes, the brightest I've ever seen before. But from what Tate said he is one of the most loyal, he'll turn his back on anybody, even his family, for his boys.

The name sounds familiar, that's what I tell Tate when she texts me back, apparently his family are huge movie producers. I wasn't expecting that.

Carter Beckett, Tate sends me the name and points to him, telling me to stay the fuck away from him with no explanation. I glance over at the boy again; he's just as big as Asher and on the football team.

There's a darkness emanating from his dark blue eyes that creeps me out.

Noah Blackwood is the one that I met earlier today, he's the nicest out of all the male God's in this school with brown hair and hazel eyes. Tate says that his family is heavily involved in politics, that his dad is a senator and might run for President. Their family opened up Black-wood Academy, so I guess there's that, too.

The popular girls that I pissed off are in the front row. I didn't even notice them until Tate pointed them out. I really don't need her to tell me about the queen bitches, I can guess.

Throughout the class I eventually learn their first names: Paisley, Palmer and Megan.

Paisley and Palmer are the only two that keep looking back and giving me death glares as hard as they can. A couple times I've giggled thinking if they're not careful, they're going to end up shitting their pants with the amount of energy they're using to strain their faces at me.

Surprisingly enough, Asher gives me a lot of room,

maybe because we're in school now. Hopefully, I don't even have to worry about him messing with me or giving me problems, like he did before at my house.

All I know is that I want to stay away from him as much as possible. I don't want to be associated with this guy at all, especially after what happened with me and Tate. *What this guy is capable of.*

If I ever got scared or needed an extra incentive to keep people away from me, I would just mention my last name, but that's not possible here. If anyone finds out who I am, then *he'll* find me to finish the job.

Even if students found out who I am, I don't think it'd make that much of a difference. The Romano's and the Delano's are evenly matched, by power, money, and prestige.

I just need to keep myself unnoticeable and far away from all of these alphas to stay safe and unrecognizable.

"Thank you everybody, I will see you tomorrow. Make sure you're fully prepared for this class and study the notes that I have listed. You can find the link in your email I'm going to send everyone after this class." Mrs. Harris said, happy to be done with us.

Tate and I were already packed up and ready as soon as she dismissed us. We shot straight for the door when the bell rang, neither one of us wanted to stick around and talk to any of those people we're trying to avoid.

By the time lunch rolls around my stomach so growling so loudly, I knew a few of the students heard it and chuckled. One girl even gave me a pity smile, hers is probably growling just as loud as mine. Luckily, we were able to get to the cafeteria before most of the other students.

There were so many choices and a lot of this shit was made to order. If we wanted, we could even go sit in the area where waiters will take our orders and bring it to us. That would take way too long, and I'm freaking starving.

We both order cheeseburgers and fries in the line, plus I got a huge salad to go with it.

No one has really claimed their tables this year, but from what I remember about schools, tables are already claimed, the hierarchy of the school sits where they rightfully belong, and thankfully Tate knows where those seats are.

We pick an area far away from where the popular kids sit, this area hasn't been claimed, which is the perfect place to hide and be unnoticed. In this area you can't really see as much action or know what's happening and you sure as hell won't be seen by anybody else. This is definitely not a table for students that want to rise up during their high school years, this is perfect for us.

We eat in silence for a few minutes, then Tate blurts out, "Asher moved in with me."

"What?" I'm shocked by this statement. Tate's living in a nice house, but it's nothing like what she's used to living in. I have no idea whose house it is, she still hasn't told me yet.

"He threatened if I told you what was going on, he would let my brothers know where I was." Tate looks heartbroken and defeated.

I give her a pity smile, which I try to mask by putting food in my mouth. The tears start rolling down Tate's face. "Why can't they just leave me alone?" She asks on a sob.

"You know how families are. If you're born into this life, you'll always be in this life." I say as she snaps her head towards me as I shrug my shoulders. She's probably wondering how I know this. "I watched a lot of TV, I know stuff." I gave her a wink as we go back to eating.

We have five minutes of peace until the full horde of students start to stumble in, laughing and talking excitedly.

In walk the elite Gods of Blackwood Academy, followed right behind them by the elite bitches. Then there has to be at least two hundred students coming in after them, all giddy and excited.

Tate sinks down a little bit more in her seat trying to remain invisible.

Both of us turn our attention back to the crowd as the popular students cut their way to the front of the line. Walker and Noah grab Paisley and Palmer and start to spin them in the air, those girls are screaming and laughing with fake excitement.

Half of the students in the cafeteria are laughing with them while the other half just don't give a fuck.

Once they've all got their food, they make their way to the tables. The boys have trays piled high with different versions of greasy heart attacks while the girls enjoy salads with nothing in them or on them, and a bottle of water.

Everyone's waiting to see where Asher will sit, then they're going to follow him as usual.

In my gut I feel a little pity towards him. What person

in their right mind would want to have to go through this every day? They just want to relax and have a good day at school without everybody following their every move. Matching everything they do, kissing their ass so bad that when they come up for air, they're face is brown, disgusting.

Asher locks eyes with me and heads in our direction. It didn't even hit me that he could be looking for us. The boy was looking around the cafeteria for a few minutes, what else could he be looking for?

"Oh God," Tate cries watching them head our way as she shakes her head.

"This year is going to suck," I mumble out.

CHAPTER 11

AVERY

Both of us sink low putting our heads down and letting our hair cover our face, not that it's going to help.

Neither one of us want to be noticed, we want to eat in peace and quiet and hide for the rest of the year if that's possible, but obviously life has a different vision than we do.

I glance up and notice the wicked smile that's on Asher's face as he walks up to our sanctuary, our hiding spot.

"Tate, Avery," he states as he nods to his group of followers. Noah and Walker happily do his bidding as they walk over and grab our plates, then start following Asher back to the table he picks out.

"Fuck," Tate growls as she slowly gets up and grabs her belongings, and I do the same. What else can we do but accept our fate? There will be other chances to stand up for ourselves but today is not it. The first day of school, everyone is looking for easy prey.

Asher has a seat right next to him available. The only other seat that's left open is next to Carter.

Tate takes that spot as I'm forced to move over next to Asher. I wasn't paying attention as we were walking over here, but apparently the whole cafeteria has their eyes on us.

They're probably shocked that the new girl made it to the popular table with the football players and cheerleaders.

Most people know that Asher and Tate are related, especially since he made her change her name back to Mancini.

It's hard to eat as everyone's eyes stay on me. I know I shouldn't care about it, but I just have the feeling that food is going to drop out of my mouth. I'm going to drool, just something gross that they can use against me later, and damn, I'm so hungry. I just want to go back to my hiding spot but we both know that it's worthless to even try right now. Tate and I are both fighters but when you want to remain invisible, fighting is not an option. We're just praying that these guys get bored and don't need us around anymore.

It shouldn't be that hard because Paisley hasn't taken her eyes off me. She keeps trying to send me a message with her glare, 'you're going to die when I get you alone.' I laugh at her, of course it was silent and very invigorating to see her expression change.

I imagine nobody has ever challenged this girl. They probably just let her walk all over them, trying to remain invisible. Basically, they're playing dead, so they're not kicked anymore.

Asher wraps his arm around me, melting me into his body. His head leans into the curve of my neck, as he inhales deeply.

"I missed you baby," he purrs and rubs his hand down my back pushing between the seat and my sweater. Thankfully, he doesn't go down extremely far, but it's enough to terrify me.

I've been down this road before, and I definitely don't plan on going back. I want nothing to do with a made man. Technically he's not a made man anymore, he's actually the boss which makes things even worse.

A nineteen-year-old boss, how awesome is that? Even better that he's got his eyes on me. I just got to figure out how to get them off.

I do feel something when I'm sitting so close curled to his side. I'd rather be dead before I have to admit that. My female hormones are blaring, and Asher is just fucking gorgeous, it's like a fantasy come true. I understand why a lot of the girls are looking at him. Some of them are probably legit not trying to reach the social hierarchy, but just because he's hot and they want to be with him.

Asher grabs my hamburger and breaks off a piece trying to feed it to me.

That just makes me snap and lose my shit, he's acting like we've been together for ages, that we're undeniably lovers.

"Fuck off," I growl out as I try to smack his hand away.

He laughs and then puts my food back on the plate. The cafeteria is still silently watching us.

What the hell is wrong with these people? They're so obsessed over the stupidest things. If they had a taste of this life, or even knew what it entailed, they would run as far as they could.

I've lost almost everything, I want out of this life more than anyone.

The defining moment for me was when I realized I don't want to be the heiress to the Romano Empire. I want to be a normal girl, I want to have a small house with a white picket fence and a husband who loves me, one that I'm not going to have to worry about dying every time he leaves the house.

I start to eat again as Asher semi leaves me alone. I know things are definitely not over between us, that he's just getting started.

If I knew he was going to the same school and that he would see me every day, I would've been gone. He left me broken in my family home, just so he could fuck with me later. I really have no clue what this man wants with me.

For some reason, maybe I just attract all the assholes, they're naturally drawn to me. *Great.*

He doesn't stop touching me, but he lets me eat in peace. At least he's not jerking me to his side anymore or running his hand down my back towards my ass.

I keep glancing at Tate, and then she keeps side eyeing Carter but never fully looking at him, I wonder what that's about.

I zone out everybody and everything. There still twenty minutes till lunch is over. An overwhelming urge tells me to run and get away, but I'm not going to leave Tate sitting here alone.

"Asher," one of the football jocks struggles to get

Asher's attention. "Is it true what the news says that the Mancini's have waged war against the Romano's?"

My hand freezes halfway up to my mouth. I was not expecting this. Yes, the Romano's are huge and into a bunch of shit that's not exactly innocent or legal, but for God's sake, the Romano's are on the other side of the freaking country.

I know the moment I go pale, I can feel all the warmth drain from my face. Do they know who I am? Is this some kind of game to see what I'll do or make me struggle?

I glance around but nobody notices or looks at me, they're just all waiting for Asher to comment.

I take a huge breath filling my lungs with much needed air. Thankfully, nobody knows who I am.

"All the Romano's do is talk shit, they're more bark than bite, and we plan to expunge that," Asher growls with no emotion on his face.

He goes back to eating for a couple minutes as everyone around the table waits to hear what else he has to say, but no one will dare to speak now. Why should I care? Why would he be blatantly talking about business and family matters, bosses don't do this, it's weird. If everyone knew who I was, I would point this out to him. Right now, my hidden identity is important.

I can see my grandfather shaking his head at him as he directly defies our moral code, it's like he doesn't give a shit.

"I have a meeting with the head of the Romano family next week to see what we can come up with. Right now, it's not a big deal, we're just letting everything play out. You can let your parents know that."

The guy that originally asked the question in the first place gives Asher a nod in understanding. I wonder who his parents are, shit, I don't even know this dude's name. I make a mental note to ask Tate later in case my grandfather needs to know.

Tate can see how uncomfortable I am. Thankfully she thinks it's for a different reason as she stands up and grabs her stuff and goes over and grabs my arm, pulling me from the cafeteria. Asher made a jerking move to grab my arm but then stopped as Tate chimed in, "if you touch her, I will fucking end you right here."

Surprise covers his face as Asher gives us both a cruel smirk as Tate pulls me out into the hallway.

We look at each other for a second and then I mumble out, "this year is going to suck balls, bad."

Tate wraps her arm in mine as we both walk to our next class. We might be early but at least we're not with them anymore.

I nod in the direction of a bathroom that's empty. It's going to be at least five minutes until class starts and everybody will wait till the last minute before they leave. I guess those extra few seconds are irreplaceable when you're with your friends or ogling one of the guys you got a crush on.

Thankfully, Tate lets me go in by myself, she's probably heading to her locker.

I barely make it in the door before the tears start to flow. I say a silent thank you that I didn't bother with makeup today. That's all I need is to spend several minutes fixing my face.

I shake my head hiding myself in one of the stalls. I

cannot go through this again. I can't deal with everything that happened before. I've already lost everything. For some strange freaking reason, I attract the worst kind of men. A marked man. A made man. The freaking boss.

I consider myself a strong woman with my training plus everything I've gone through to know what to do to protect myself mentally and physically. This time I don't know if I can get away from him.

Asher keeps looking at me like I'm a piece of meat, something to devour and possess, but I'm not. I'm not somebody's prize. I want somebody who loves me, preferably somebody like an accountant. *Someone boring.*

Even though he hasn't stated his intentions, deep down inside I know. Since he doesn't know who I am, there can only be one thing, *me.*

I need to look up what is going on with the Mancini's and the Romano's, then I need to call my freaking grandfather. He said only contact him in a life-or-death situation, this is definitely one of those situations. A war between two families will mean a lot of deaths.

My grandfather might have me spy for him, or he'll remove me from the school, since the Romano's are such a huge crime family. If there is going to be a war, I'm on the wrong side of the country.

I know my friend wants nothing to do with her family, she wants out of this world as much as I do. I can only imagine her face when she finds out that I'm a Romano.

I shake my head getting all the thoughts out of it. Right now, I need to focus on the present and not the fact that I might have to tell my friend who I am. 'Hey you can come with us even though our families are fighting, we'll have so much fun.'

Luckily, I was able to exit the bathroom as the three bitches come in. They didn't spot me with my head down. By the time they noticed it was too late, I was out the door. I'm fairly sure they want their pound of flesh for what I did to them, which won't happen. One day we'll fight out our differences. Too bad they don't know just how good of a fighter I am.

I need to plan. The first thing I'm going to do when I get a chance is call my grandfather. If I have to, I'll beg to be moved somewhere else, somewhere our enemies will never expect. States like Louisiana and Alabama. I'm the hidden link in an extremely dangerous game that's about to start. I lift my head knowing that a Romano can't be beat and walk my happy ass to my next class.

CHAPTER 12

Asher

The shock on Avery's face was worth not letting Tate say anything to her for over a week. I'll admit one of the main reasons I did it is just so that I could see Avery's reaction. I wouldn't have it any other way, it was perfect.

The main reason I didn't want her to know was because I didn't want Avery to have a chance to make other arrangements. I don't know that much about Avery yet, but I know that she doesn't live with her parents. She lives with family members. I have no clue what happened to her parents, and I'd be lying if I said I didn't want to know, because I do. I want to know every single thing about this girl.

I want to know what makes her tick, I want to know what turns her on. I want to know her favorite foods, her favorite drinks, everything, and I sure as shit can't find that out if she leaves.

Not allowing Tate to say anything gave me some extra time to figure out more about Avery. Shockingly, nothing came up. I cannot find shit on this girl. No social media accounts, nothing. It's like she hasn't even existed before the school year.

Which is all the more intriguing to me. I need to know every single thing, no matter how damaging it is about Avery.

If she found out I was enrolling in Blackwood Academy she would've left, I had no issue getting enrolled. What were they going to do? Try and turn me away, I fucking rule the East Coast.

I don't even know if she'd have somewhere else to go. I've had guys watching her house, but nobody else has shown up and left, except for those that own the house. They were only there for hardly any amount of time.

This girl is just as alone as I am, and I want to know why.

A lot of the guys slap me on the back as everyone makes their way out of the last class. This would be easier for me if Avery was here with me, but she's not.

I'm not too worried about it though, everyone talks and watches. With what went down at lunch, everyone knows who Avery Stone is now. I could ask any of these idiots where she is, and they'd give me her exact location.

I don't want my desperation to overtake me, but I feel the need to be constantly around her. I head down to her locker, which, conveniently after this morning, is only a few down from mine.

I was assigned one on the other side of the hallway where most of the popular kids like to be. They're able to see everything, who is coming and going from both sides of the school. It even makes it awkward for the new attendees, the younger class, because they have to walk by them all the time. A break in between classes is an entertainment show for the popular kids.

As I get closer to my locker and more people notice me walking by, the hallways go silent, watching and waiting to see what will happen. If these idiots would focus more on their lives right now, everything would be better for them. It's like I'm living in a fucking soap opera.

It does get to me after a while. Many people would jump at the opportunity to be idolized, but not me. It's exhausting. I have to deal with this shit enough when I'm out there in the real world. Now I've been gifted with a younger version of idiots.

Next year they'll have their very own leader. One of the juniors will do the same thing I do, but maybe he will enjoy it. There's pretty much no way to stop it, there's always going to be a hierarchy, even at the inner-city schools.

The top of the social circle will be more important here because of how famous the kids are. One of these kids is the offspring of the biggest supermodel of our century. There's enough senators' kids and even kids higher up on the political ladder, but in this school those people are a dime a dozen.

Avery and Tate both have their heads pushed together in the opening of their locker talking about something. Luckily for me Tate's my niece, and even in the school setting she can't disrespect me or raise alarm.

"How are my favorite girls today?" I say as I throw my arm over both of their shoulders, squeezing them tight to me. Tate cringes as her body tenses up and she stands ramrod straight. Avery leans into me just a little bit, but not too much. I'm not sure if this girl knows what to do with herself or maybe she's trying to take the attention from Tate.

This pisses me off, but my girl has a big heart and she's trying to shoulder the burden so that her friend doesn't have to. Tate can't say anything to me, but Avery can.

Avery and I are fucking meant to be together and nothing can stop this, definitely not Tate or any of the other idiots around the school.

"Asher," Tate snarls out as she easily gets out of my hold. I was latching onto her as hard as I am Avery. To the bystanders that are watching us, it'll look like Tate's being sweet and maneuvers around me to get her stuff. That girl got away from me like I've got the fucking plague and I'm about to infect her and everyone else. She's the only one who can stop it.

With Tate out of the way and Avery still curled under my arm, I push my girl back up against the locker and rest my forearms on both sides of her head.

"We're having a small, intimate get together at our house." I say to Avery as I look over to Tate, giving her a wink. I'm waiting to see if Tate's going to battle knowing that people are coming to her house on the first day of school.

Tate deserves this. I've had my guys searching for the owners of the house for months. For some reason, someone wants it to remain hidden. I will find out. It'll take longer, but eventually I'll know who has a nice set up for my niece. This fancy ass house is above her pay grade when she's not with family.

We've had several fights on this but no matter what I do, even if I threaten to call her brothers to come out here and take care of this, she refuses to tell me who the owner is. I thought it would be easy to find the owner, but no such luck, even using Devon. There's got to be thousands of shell companies that are bouncing back and forth, throwing us off the trail.

Whoever owns this house definitely does not want to be found, by anyone.

"Oh, I really don't want to get together right now, so I'll just go home. Tate and I already planned on doing some homework together." I can tell how nervous Avery is. I should try to make her feel more comfortable, but this game we're playing excites me more than anything else has in a while. Even crushing the arms or the skull of guys that have wronged me and my family isn't as exciting. *This woman will be the death of me.*

I neutralize my expression and make sure that she can tell I'm okay with that. "That's fine, we'll just bring the get together over to your house. I know that the Stones' are rarely ever there."

Avery's eyes open wide with what looks like a little bit of fear, she definitely doesn't want us all over there. *She doesn't want me over there.* I'm not even sure she would care about other people. It would be a good opportunity for them both to meet more people outside their little group of two.

Her face changes from one of fear to one of anger, extreme anger. I should be happy that this girl doesn't carry, if she did I'm sure I'd have a hole in my head right now.

"Fine," she snaps out at me. "I'll go over to your stupid little after school party, but I'm riding with Tate."

I should've just grabbed her by the back of the head, squeezing my fist around the roots tightly, not letting her move an inch from me as I drag her to my car. But unfortunately, I keep hearing Doppler's head in my voice. If I terrorize the girl, she's never willingly going to be mine.

Yeah, the game's a little bit fun, but my obsession needs more from her. Any other girl I would've just shrugged my shoulders and walked the fuck away, but not Avery.

I give her a wink totally ignoring Tate and say, "I'll see you there."

Both of the girls leave immediately after our conversation and arrive at the house before me and the rest of the group. I was honest, I said it wasn't going to be a big group gathering. I don't have full control of his house yet, since I don't know whose it is, I don't want bigger problems later.

Thankfully, this house is fucking stocked with every kind of alcohol. The owner is my kind of guy, or girl.

After an hour of hanging out, drinking with the other popular people from Blackwood Academy, I sent Tate a message. Those girls can't keep hiding forever.

Tate: get down here right now or we're all coming up to you and bring your friend.

A few minutes later both girls finally join our little get together. There has to be about thirty people here. My crew and the bitch crew, plus a bunch of football players and cheerleaders. Tate and Avery did not connect with any of these people, so my watching them is entertainment for me.

I thought I would enjoy this a lot more, but honestly, I'm bored off my ass being back in school. Everything is in capable hands back in New York and the people that are covering for me will call if anything comes up. Surprisingly enough it's been quiet.

My girls are sitting on a little sofa loveseat that's far away from all the others. Neither one of them are drinking, they just have bottles of water. I need to rectify that for them.

"Liam, give them something to drink. Something a lot stronger than what they're drinking now." Liam has a spark in his eye, he knows exactly what I'm trying to do.

He takes a drink over to them with a knowing glance my way as he follows my line of sight. Neither one of them should be shocked.

Avery is making this fucking hard and I really need to get my dick wet. There's at least ten girls that keep hovering around me, they'll do whatever I want. One girl sat in my lap without getting permission, I didn't even notice right away. I'm too busy staring at the one I really want, so I popped that bitch off me.

"Hey baby," the nasal sound makes me cringe as Paisley comes in and presses her body right against mine sitting on the edge of the armchair that I'm in.

My first thought is to push her away, but this is more entertaining. I'm curious to see if Avery has any kind of spark towards me. I could feel how she trembled, and I knew she was wet when we were at her house before. No reasonable girl is going to do anything when they're being held against their will.

Paisley runs a pointed manicured fingernail down my chest. It feels like she's trying to cut into my soul, which wouldn't be shocking from the bitch she truly is. "Fuck off, Paisley." She grunts and gives me a 'fuck you' look. One that tells me this isn't the end as she stomps her skinny ass back towards her friends that are hanging out with the football crew.

I would have the bitch stay on my lap or let her blow me right now, but Avery is not even paying attention. Both her and Tate are huddled in conversation again.

This is such a new feeling to me and I'm going to take Doppler's word as I avoid contact with her. I believe the deadly giant when he tells me to give her some time just so she can warm up to me a little bit. After he said that he started laughing. Can anyone really fucking warm up to me?

I ISOLATE MYSELF IN THE CORNER TRYING TO TAKE IN everyone around me, but my eyes naturally focus back to her, she's the only one I'm interested in looking at. I don't care about all these other idiots, the party is just a reason for us to be together and make sure she's more comfortable.

I keep having one of the guys take alcohol over to them whenever their drinks are low. Normally I wouldn't let them take anything from anybody, but I've been watching the whole time, these four guys I trust with my life, and Liam even works for me.

After about an hour of them sipping their drinks, I believe they're both on the third, everyone is relaxed a lot more. Music is pumping throughout the house and everybody's dancing in different spots. Thank God Paisley finally landed herself a jock. I think it's the fucking quarterback or something, I honestly don't give a shit. Her and her friends are dancing in the middle of the living room, since the furniture was pushed back.

My mouth opens and I quickly close it as I watch a very buzzed Avery and Tate make their way out to the middle of the living room and start dancing.

"Holy fucking shit," I mumble as I watch the moves that Avery has. She's fucking hot. I can tell this girl likes to dance. What I can also tell is that she's got the attention of every freaking jock in the room...

I haven't made a huge stand on making Avery off-limits, but I have a feeling I would need to do that soon, along with Tate. "Fuck," I swear, still sitting on the couch.

One of the linebackers, I think his name is Johnny, is dancing with Avery. Both of his parents are huge and successful vloggers, but that's it, there's nothing else more interesting about him. He is one big fucking bastard if he thinks Avery wants him dancing with her. She's too small, she wouldn't be able to fight him off.

I don't know as much about this guy as I should. I can still hear Doppler's words in my head, keeping me from jumping up and killing him right now. I do sit on the edge of the couch just in case I need to rip him limb from limb for touching what's mine.

I have this whole freaking couch to myself. When any of the girls or anyone except for one of my men try to sit down, I snap and tell them to get the fuck away.

Johnny is right behind Avery and starts matching her dancing. They're both grinding their hips and Avery has her hands above her head, but Johnny doesn't. His hands are moving up and down her arms, moving slowly towards her waist, cradling her hips tight as he pulls her into him. Avery's face widens in surprise. Bastard is fucking hard.

Johnny moves fast turning Avery around as he crashes his mouth to hers. The whole room stops, even the dancers. Everyone glances from them to me.

Everyone in this fucking house, most likely the school, knows my intentions with Avery. They can see how I look at her, but apparently not the jock yet. Maybe he knows exactly what he's doing, maybe he wants me to beat the shit out him.

My guys are heading in my direction most likely trying to stop what's about to start, but they're too far away, they'll never make it here in time.

It doesn't matter though. I told them to stand the fuck down with a wave of my hand. I need everyone in this room to know exactly that this girl's off-limits, that she's mine. Everybody here is a fucking chatterbox of gossip. Word will get around the school fast that Avery is off-limits.

I kick the tank of a linebacker in the back of his knees letting him fall. He's up in two seconds ready to fight.

When he spins around getting ready to lay one on me, he notices who I am and freezes. "Why the fuck are you on my girl?" I growl out as I grab his shirt in my fists, yanking him towards my face.

His hands go up in a surrender motion. "Fuck man, I didn't know. I would've never been near her if I knew she was yours."

I rain punch after punch down on him in the short amount of time I have. "You don't fucking touch what's mine."

It doesn't last for long before my guys are pulling me off and telling Johnny to get the fuck out. Several of the other football players leave with him but not all of them. I know where their loyalty lies.

Before the football players that are leaving make it to the door and for the ones that are currently looking at her, I make a point to look everyone in the eyes. Avery and Tate have currently plastered themselves against the wall, staying away from all the action. I smile a little bit because they both are still drinking.

"Avery Stone is off-limits," I say as I keep my eyes glued to her making sure she understands this, too. "She is mine, I will kill any motherfucker that touches her."

There are a few sighs and disappointed looks from the girls and several people shrug. Most people knew this, they've been able to watch and see my interest in the new girl that suddenly showed up during senior year when nobody's allowed to even join after freshman year.

Avery looks disgusted with me and both girls on the other side of the room are only a straight shot to the front door, which is what they do.

I start to quickly walk after them as Carter holds me back. "You need to let her go. This 'stay in my bed' glare works on some girls, but I have a feeling it won't work on her," Carter whispers in my ear, only loud enough for just two people around us to hear.

"Fuck," I scream as loud as I can as I grab the nearest bottle of alcohol out of some loser's hand and throw it against the wall.

Within five minutes I end my own party. Everyone is gone except for my guys. Paisley and her fucking annoying friends try to stay but thankfully Liam kicks them out.

"Don't be a caveman," Carter says as he looks over his shoulder at me, the rest of the guys walk out of the house with him. When I get overly pissed off, it's best to leave me alone and they all know this.

I want to fight,

I want to kill,

I want to destroy.

But for now, I need to calm down and give Avery more time. I'm taking what's mine tomorrow.

At least knowing this I relax a little more. I should be able to sleep tonight knowing that I'm going to get what I want tomorrow.

Some of my guards will be watching the girls to make sure they're safe for tonight and there's always men outside Avery's house. I don't even bother forcing my ass to move upstairs to my room. I just sleep the night away on the couch.

CHAPTER 13

AVERY

I groan as I grab my head, lifting my sorry ass out of bed. I can't believe I drank that much last night, my head is pounding. There's a little construction crew in my brain that's exploding stuff trying to get out.

After I quit my moaning, I turn to my side to see if Tate is still passed out, the bed is cold, she's been up for a while.

There's a lot of noise, dishes and pans are violently smashing against each other. The smell coming up the stairs is absolute greasy heaven, someone's making breakfast. I'm not sure what woke me up, the noise or the smell, either way my stomach is growling.

Some much-needed pain reliever and greasy food will take away my hangover, giving me a clear head so I can concentrate on what the fuck we're going to do about Asher. He seems to have an imaginary hold on both of us. I know he wants me, and he wants Tate to fall in line with the family.

At a slow pace I make my way downstairs. I completely ignore Tate's happy ass, she seems to be dancing as she cooks. I go over to the cabinet that has the Tylenol and other pain relievers in it. She notices me out of the corner of her eye and goes back to what she was previously doing.

I love that more than anything about her, I don't want to talk when I feel like shit. Tate even serves me a huge plate of breakfast. "I might need to make you my girlfriend or my bitch. Doesn't really matter as long as I can eat like this every day."

Tate snorts and continues to shovel food into her mouth. That girl eats like she hasn't seen a meal in ten days.

"How are you so fucking chirpy?" I ask. I know my eyes are shining right now, I'm starting to feel better.

"No matter how much I drink, even if it's a little bit, I make sure to take something like aspirin or whatever I can get my hands on before I go to sleep. Plus, I drink a full bottle of water. I never have problems the next day."

Shit, I think to myself. She could've fucking told me that last night.

Both of us sit in comfortable silence ignoring the elephant that's definitely in the room, getting bigger as every minute goes by, waiting to explode.

I'm the first one to give in. "Who owns the house?" I ask looking at my food. I didn't even manage to make it through a quarter plate, I'm stuffed and I'm feeling better.

"I can't say," she answers, the happiness in her eyes fading to one of sadness.

"Why don't you just tell Asher who owns it? Maybe he'll leave you alone then. Hopefully, he'll just move out." I watch her eyes to see if she is even considering this. I've asked her several times who the owner is, and I get the same answer every time.

Tate just shakes her head no. I'm not going to push anymore, we're all dealing with this crap. We both need to avoid Asher as much as we can.

"What about you? For some reason, my uncle seems obsessed with your ass." Tate smiles as she says the end. We both know it's not a happy situation, but for some reason it's kind of funny.

"Asher Mancini rules all of the east coast from my understanding, and I can't go through this again." I pinch my lips together as I realize what I just said. Tate knows nothing about my past, and I intend to keep it that way, especially since the Mancini's might be starting a fight with Romano's. I quickly amend the situation, "I just can't let my heart get broken again."

Tate nods like she's been there and understands what I'm going through. I doubt if she does, but who knows. She doesn't know who I am and I sure as hell never figured out that she was a Mancini until Asher came in our lives.

The tears start to well up in my eyes as I realize one day she will find out who I am. Will she think this was planned? I hope not, hopefully she just knows that it's me and understands that I've got secrets of my own. For God's sake I'm hiding from somebody that killed my family.

At least I found out that my grandfather's still alive. If I would've been more prominent and joined family affairs, I probably would've known before. I'm heartbroken over this, it shouldn't have taken that long for me to meet my grandfather. So many years have been wasted.

But it's not really like Vito Romano is going to be one for taking his granddaughter to an amusement park, no, I doubt that would happen, but dinners and just being around him would've been all that mattered. Time is all we needed.

We both clean up the kitchen in more silence. We should be excited and having fun, our senior year just started, but we're down and depressed. I've got to figure out a way to change our situation.

I laugh a little to myself as I realize the one person making this all happen is Asher Mancini. If we deal with him, everything should be fine.

Tate gives me a hug as I head back to my house.

The inevitable is rearing its ugly head and I know that I need to have a long conversation with my grandfather. I'm not supposed to get a hold of him unless it's a matter of life and death, but he needs to know who I go to school with, and what I've been hearing. Even though I don't want to admit it, I probably need to leave California and head back to the East Coast or somewhere stupid down south, to stay safe.

If I stay here things are going to blow up and it's not going to be good. As long as Asher is taking so much interest in me other people will be, too. It's only a matter of time until they realize that they go to school with the supposed enemy. Since Asher is a Mancini and at the top of the hierarchy in the school, that's what's important. A single Romano in the school is nothing but a death sentence.

I walk back upstairs to my room and grab my cellphone to give Arya a call.

"Is everything okay?" I don't even think the phone made it through the full ring before she answered.

"Everything's is fine, but I need to talk to grandpa now." My voice is low as I say this. Both of us know what it means, that something is seriously wrong.

"Can I help with anything?" I want to be able to tell her everything, but I don't want to put this on her shoulders, either.

"No, it's something that grandpa has to take care of. But please don't worry, it's all going to be fine."

Arya is quiet, her and I both know that if I need to call my grandfather that it's not going to be fine, there's a serious problem.

"We can leave right now Avery, Garrett is finishing a meeting and we don't have anything for a couple days. We can make it back by late tonight or tomorrow morning." I shake my head even though she can't see me. From my understanding both of them are in London, and they hardly get enough rest as it is.

"I promise Arya, everything is as fine as it can be. If there are any more problems, I'll call you. I know that if it were a bad situation grandpa wouldn't want you to be here anyway." I sigh, I really don't know how to make her feel better.

"Okay sweetie, please keep in touch so I know that you're okay. You can call or text anytime, day or night." Arya takes a breather and I hear sniffling. It makes my heart swell to know how much this woman cares about me. "Keep your phone on you, your grandfather should be calling anytime."

"Thank you, I love you guys," I say as I hang up the phone. I think it might break me if I hear her say it back.

I had planned on taking a shower right after I talked to Arya but my phone rings less than a minute later from a blocked number.

My grandpa's trying to keep me hidden and out of sight, so it's not like he can call on a familiar number, something that I have a record of in case someone gets my phone.

"Avery," my grandfather growls out. Vito Romano is one scary ass mother fucker. Just him saying my name alone terrifies the shit out of me. I've never heard him talk this way before, but then again, I haven't known him that long, I can see why he's so high up.

"I'm sorry to bother you," I mutter out.

"What's going on? Arya wasn't able to tell me anything, and we both know that you're not supposed to call unless there's an emergency." My grandfather growls. "Did Luca find you?"

"W-what, I thought Luca was in jail?" My heart is racing, it feels like it's going to burst out of my chest in a second and splatter on our immaculate clean floor.

"He made bail two days ago, but he doesn't know where you're at. If it's not Luca, then why are you calling?" Grandpa's voice is still low and threatening, but since he is family and obviously worried about me, I don't feel like shitting my pants anymore.

I keep the tears at bay, I can't believe my parent's killer made bail. I need to calm down and I need to let Grandpa know about the Mancini's, specifically Asher. Luca killed both my parents and tried to kill me. How is he able to go free?

"Avery, I'm in a time crunch right now, I need you to tell me what's going on."

I shake my head, I'll let myself panic when I get off the phone. "Asher Mancini goes to my school."

My grandfather says nothing at first, I'm not sure if he knew where Asher was. "Stay away from him Avery, he's not a good man, one of the worst."

"At lunch yesterday I heard them talking about how there's gonna be a war between the Mancini's and the Romano's." I grab my hand and squeeze the digits, willing myself not to freak out.

"That's just a bunch of bullshit that's going around. A couple of the made men got into a scuffle over a girl. This will be addressed, at a meeting here in a few days." My grandfather stays quiet just for second. "I don't want to let all this stuff get to you. I want you to relax and stay far away from everything. I'll take care of this, don't worry about any of the Mancini's." He sighs, I have a feeling that if I were able to see him right now he'd be running his hands up and down his face trying to calm his nerves as much as I am. I love how we're both trying to be strong for the other one.

"I'll try to relax as much as I can, I just thought you'd want to know." I say waiting for him to start screaming or yelling at me. I don't know why I expected it but for some reason I just do.

"I'm glad you called, and keep me informed through Arya, the same way we just did. But more than anything stay away from Asher Mancini and if you see or hear from Luca, I want to be called instantly."

I don't want to feel like I'm a spy or anything like that, especially since Tate is also a Mancini. "What happens if I hear something important like something they might do to you guys?"

"If it's bad or threatening, have Arya get a hold of me. Listen to me now Avery, whatever you have to do, make sure you avoid any kind of interaction you might have with Asher or Luca."

"I will, I love you grandpa." The tears threaten to spill, besides the Stones he's the only family I have left.

"I love you, too, stay safe." He barely finishes getting out the last word before the line is disconnected.

I send a text message to Arya letting her know everything is okay. *Everything is not okay though.*

Both Arya and grandpa sounded exhausted when I talked to them. This whole situation is stressful enough, it's even harder trying to keep me hidden. I have a feeling if he told the Stones that Luca is out on bail, they'd both be on their way home. The Stones work so hard there's no reason that they should have to sit here and babysit me and fall behind at work.

I still have one hidden defense and Luca didn't even know that I've been training since I was really young. Asher might suspect after what I did to Doppler, but I don't think he knows, either.

Everything is starting to change, my life and the lives of my family members are on the line. There's no way I'm going to let anything happen to anybody.

It's time for me to fight back. I think as I get my ass in gear, I might be hungover, but I still have school.

CHAPTER 14

Avery

When I entered the kitchen the next morning, I pretend that my mom is behind the counter making a shit ton of breakfast foods. The comforting feeling warms my blood, making me feel like I can get through this day.

Of course, there's nobody back there, not even Arya. I don't want this warm feeling to go away. I grab myself an apple from a fruit basket that always seems to be filled, even when nobody's here, how weird. Maybe I just don't eat enough fruit to notice and they just refill it when they come back. It warms my heart a little bit because I realize every time that they're home for the night, they go to the grocery store for me.

I take a deep breath as I go out onto the porch and wait for Tate to arrive. There's so much more at stake here than simply going to school, my life is on the line. No matter what happens and no matter what I do, I can't let them find out my true identity.

If any of the Mancini's find out who I am, especially

120

after all this talk about a war that's going to take place with the Romano's, I'll be well and truly fucked.

I take deep breaths as I watch the cars coming up and down the street, I actually feel like I'm getting sick. I could just stay home today, but then I'll have to deal with this shit tomorrow. Nothing will change, nothing will get better unless I face the music now.

I could just be worrying over nothing, I think as a smile goes across my face. Nobody probably has even a clue and they're not even close to figuring out exactly who I am.

I just need to go back to remaining invisible. I sigh, that'll never happen. Asher Mancini is not going to stop until he has what he wants, which is me.

A brief thought flashes through my head about being honest with him. Letting Asher know that I'm hiding and if he could just give me space, maybe after senior year we can date. I can imagine the wheels turning in his head, he'd work nonstop until he figured out who I was.

My girl pulls up in front of the house. She is all smiles and happiness, it's kind of annoying, but I still love her.

"Hey, what's wrong?" Tate asks as I slide myself into her cute and sporty little BMW. I wonder if her housemate or whoever she's renting the house from gave her this BMW also.

I sigh and look out the window. I know that my eyes are pooling with tears. "I just wish this year would finish, like yesterday." Tate grabs my hand over the console and gives a slight squeeze. I'm not sure she's doing it to console me or if she totally agrees.

"We'll get through it, we just need to remain as invisible as we can. Under no circumstances can we bring attention to ourselves." She says the last part and moves her hand back to the steering wheel.

"That's going to be nearly impossible with Asher and his crew and let's not forget the bitch group." Tate laughs as I say the last thing.

"Keep your head up high, girl, don't let them get you down. All of them will get bored of us sooner or later, we just need to keep our wits about us until the time comes."

I laugh, "you sound like one of our teachers."

The ride to school is fairly quiet. It's exactly what I needed to get my ass to fucking relax.

Just the walk from the parking lot towards the entrance says enough about our whole situation alone. The entire school body is gawking at us. Some people straight out point as others hide behind their hands, but their eyes watch us the whole time. I wonder how that's working for them hiding what they say behind their hands like they're not gossiping about us, but they're watching our every move. I shake my head, h*igh school, yay*.

Some people look at me with jealousy and envy. The girls want to be me, or the guys just want to fuck me. Great, the claim that Asher put down has definitely gotten out and there were hardly any kids at the party. At the end of the hallway Paisley, Palmer and Megan don't look very envious, they look downright hateful, even Megan, the one that seems semi-sweet. That's only a cover though, she's in the bitch group so that's what she is.

Luckily for me first period goes by without a hitch. Out in the hall I manage to see Tate for a couple minutes before she runs off to our next class. I have to pee really bad and I'm debating going to class and then asking to use the restroom. That won't work if I don't go now, I should probably just go to the bathroom, I've been holding it too long.

I have a little over a minute before the bell rings, so I make my way to the bathroom, it's right next to my trigonometry class. The bathroom is empty as I make my way inside and run towards the closest stall.

I almost cry out in relief as I finish. How can a person not pee first thing in the morning?

As I finish washing my hands the door to the bathroom opens. Just my luck, it happens to be Paisley, Palmer and Megan.

All three of the girls are giggling about something stupid one of the football players said. It's not stupid to them, just stupid to me.

"Well look what we have here," Paisley says as she stands right in front of me when I turn around, flanked by both Palmer and Megan.

The warning bell goes off, letting us know that we have thirty seconds to make it to class. "Got to go," I say to them as sweetly as I can, showcasing my brightest smile.

Of course, nothing ever goes as planned. Right as I put my hand on the door to exit my head is pushed hard smacking against the cold harsh tile of the bathroom walls.

Oh, hell no, even though I don't want to be late for class, I need to put a few bitches in place.

I whip myself around and drop my bag, pushing up the thin sleeves of my cardigan so they don't get in the way.

I've been trained to fight multiple people, people that

are experienced. Not three high school girls that think their shit don't stink.

All three of the girls see my eyes and the hatred that flows through them, it's really just annoyance, but whatever will work. They step back, a flash of fear goes through Paisley as she quickly wills it away.

"Who the fuck touched me?" I ask as I look between all three of them. Palmer and Megan put their heads down, as Paisley gives me a smirk.

With nothing else to lose, Paisley makes her way over to me nose to nose. "You need to stay the fuck away from Asher." That is so cliché.

I sigh. "Why don't you ask him to stay away from me? I don't want him." I bend down to grab my bag, nothing's going to happen in here today. These insufferable bitches would rather fight through words than punches.

This moment in time will be one that I lecture myself on for years to come. I let myself relax thinking there was no threat, but in actuality there was a huge one.

Paisley was on my side as I bent to grab my bag. She kicked me as hard as she could with her pointed high heels. The pain was excruciating. It felt like she was able to jam me right in between the ribs. I slide down on the floor trying to catch my breath as all three of the girls start kicking anywhere they can: sides, head, everywhere.

I know I'm going to have a few bruises, but that doesn't stop the anger flowing through me, the one that wants blood. I feel like I'm some superhero as I jump up to a standing position. I feel like I've come out of being encased in cement, keeping me locked up.

All three of them gasp as they realize I'm not down for

the count. I work fast, the girls are too shocked to cover themselves or even try to get away.

I land a punch straight to Paisley's face as I hear her bones crack. She screams and I smile at the sound of her nose shattering.

Palmer was running over to help her best friend, the good minion she is. I know that bitch kicked me a few times. I smile as I punch her right at the base of the neck. I'm not planning on crushing her trachea or anything else, I just want her to be out of breath for a couple minutes. I want to scare the shit out of her.

Megan looks like she wants to pass out, even though she's the nicest one here, the bitch was still kicking me. I do a basic roundhouse kick, never leaving the floor, getting her straight on the side of the head. Her heels have to be at least 6 inches. I thought about first kicking her off her feet and letting her sprain her ankle when she lands. I can't be guaranteed that would work. If her ankle snaps, then I would for sure get suspended, but they did attack first, I was just protecting myself. These girls are bitches that cause too much trouble. I know the Dean would take my side right away, especially when he sees my bruised body and three on one.

All three girls are on the floor writhing in pain. Palmer has her cell phone out most likely calling for help or the Dean. I really hope she calls the police, I'm right in every way.

Thankfully, I don't have that much blood on me. I've got some nice bruises starting to form. I don't fucking mind war marks, especially when I won the battle.

I smile as I make my way over to the door. "You're

gonna pay for this bitch," Paisley hisses out. "You have no idea who my father is, you'll be dead by the end of the day."

"Really," I ask feigning interest and acting like I'm a little bit scared. "Maybe you should figure out who my father is. I didn't learn to fight from being on social media."

I give them all a big smile and a little wave as I walk to trigonometry late. God, I hate fucking being late.

I thought for sure I would experience some sort of euphoric high after everything that just went down, after I put the bitch crew in their place. I feel nothing like that, I'm a huge ball of nerves.

If for some reason Palmer did call the police, then I'm basically fucked. Who knows how deep they would dig. Would they be able to find out exactly who I am? *Fuck*.

It's not only that, if they did call the police then the Dean's coming now. I can't worry about this right now. My parents taught me only to worry when absolutely necessary. When the police are walking in the classroom with handcuffs ready to go, then I'll start to worry. I glance down over my body just to check my war wounds, they're pretty bad, I can't even touch my side. I want to lift my shirt to see, but I know it's not pretty.

I can breathe a little better as the morning comes to an end. I haven't run in to the three girls again, but I did see them down the hallway from my locker using makeup very religiously. Hopefully, it'll help but honestly I don't give a shit if it doesn't, they deserved it. They should wear their war wounds proud.

I stand at my locker waiting for Tate. Her happy ass

bounces up to the locker as she puts her stuff away and we head for lunch.

I want to ask what's going on and why she's so happy, but I don't want her to notice me. That was my fight, and I don't want accolades for it, I just want to go on throughout my day. The shit would keep happening unless I stand up for myself.

Just as expected after we get our lunch and try to sit at our little corner table at the far end of the cafeteria, Asher and all of his followers come right up next to us. This time instead of making us move, they pull more tables together and sit down. Several of the people run back to grab food and get everything Asher and the other guys need.

Having a waiter, I guess is cool, but overall, the whole situation would still suck. I imagine Asher would love to have quiet, to be invisible just as much as we would.

He seems to be in a good mood, maybe it would work if I was able to talk to him. He sits to my left as close as he can, while Tate sits on my other side. Students fill in the empty chairs around the tables as they talk animatedly to themselves. Paisley and her friends must've done a good job hiding everything, no one said anything about them being in a fight.

I take a drink of water watching the door to the cafeteria trying to keep my eyes away from everyone else. Paisley, Palmer and Megan walk in. The water spits out of my mouth and lands on a couple jocks across the table. I raise my hand in an 'I'm sorry' motion because I can't stop laughing. I was able to calm my ass down before I started choking.

Everyone watches me with wide eyes and then they turn and focus their attention on what I'm looking at. Tate starts to laugh and Asher chuckles very lightly. His tight group of friends don't hold it in. Liam, Walker, Carter, and Noah are full on belly laughing. It looks like they hate those bitches as much as we do.

Thankfully, the gossip doesn't start. People don't ask questions as to why Paisley's wearing pretty much a face cast over her nose. She's got two huge black eyes.

I lean into Asher. "Can I talk to you for a minute?"

"Sure baby," he says as he wraps his arm around my shoulder pulling me tightly into him.

Okay, I don't even know how to work this. I mean I like the guy, he's fucking hot and he does some weird things to my body that I never knew anyone could, but I like living better.

"I was wondering if we could be friends and hang out until the end of year." Oh my God I can't believe I just did the, 'we could be friends thing.' "That sounds horrible. What I'm trying to say is that I've got a lot on my plate and a lot of family matters, and I'm just wondering if maybe wait until we graduate, then we can start dating or something. Right now, I just want to remain invisible. I don't want to date anyone."

Asher laughs a full belly laugh and throws his head back. The cafeteria goes quiet as everybody turns around and watches. *Great.*

"That's not gonna happen baby, and I know you feel the same way I do." Maybe I do, but it doesn't matter. I refuse to start thinking about it. I refuse to daydream about him and the things he can do to me. If he only knew everything, he might just kill me with his bare hands.

I stand up to get away but at the same time, so does Asher. Everyone watches us, even Tate is frozen with a forkful of spaghetti halfway up to her mouth.

Asher tries to intimidate me, placing one hand on my hip and the other on my back. He crushes me to his body as my previous worries fall away. Oh God, his lips are so soft as he crushes them to mine, he is so demanding tasting like the Italian pizza that he just had.

All I want to do is grab his hand and lead us to a quiet room or even outside to the fifty cars in the parking lot.

Before I get too lost in myself, I push hard on his chest which gives me just a tiny bit of room. Asher is a fucking tank and regains the empty space between us instantly. Luckily for me I don't need my hands free, I maneuver my leg in between his and slam it up as hard as I can.

He screams and drops. A kick, a punch, even a slap to the balls can drop the biggest and meanest assholes out there. I bend down next to him and sneer, "get a fucking clue Asher." I'm fuming mad. I honestly don't even think this guy knows how to date. He's probably just been one that grabbed and fucked whenever he wanted to. "I'm not into you, therefore we will never happen, so back the fuck off."

Tate wraps her stuff up and we both practically run out of the cafeteria. I know I'll have to pay for my actions later, but I need to send a message to him, and all the rubberneckers. This is the only way that senior year will be livable.

Hopefully, Asher Mancini will understand.

CHAPTER 15

ASHER

I lift my ass back into my chair as one of the lower-class men brings me an ice pack for my balls. Hopefully, the fuckers will drop back down. Avery kicked me good, kicked me almost like she hated me.

What the fuck is wrong with her? I knew this girl was going to take a lot more work than the other ones, but Avery's acting like a rich spoiled brat.

Who the fuck wouldn't want to be with me? She's basically committing social suicide by what she just did. I can fuck anyone in the school that I want, including the teachers, and I happen to choose somebody that wants nothing to do with me.

I can feel the blood start to boil in my veins. This whole situation is bullshit and there's no way in hell I'm gonna let that girl get away from me.

The anger just doesn't subside, it's growing and fester-ing. All I want to do is chase her, hunt her down and fuck her right on the spot no matter where we are. I'll make sure that my come covers every inch of her body, rubbing it into her skin and her pussy. The girl is mine, she just needs to start realizing that.

I shift slightly as my balls cry out in agony. My anger is boiling right back up again.

I stand to my full height as I let everything just take over and scream, "FUCK!" All the noise in the cafeteria stops, and everyone looks at me. This isn't in amusement like previously, no, everyone looks terrified.

I just don't fucking care anymore. I start to throw the chairs from around the table in different directions. The smart ones move away, and the stupid ones just sit there and watch, shocked. Their dumb asses need to move, I'm not paying attention to where I throw anything. I honestly don't give a shit if they're too stupid to move, that's their own fault.

Anything I can find is fair game, whether it's flipping over tables or throwing backpacks and trays. This goes on for what seems like forever to me, but it probably wasn't that much. I scream, I'm not even sure what I'm screaming. The anger is clouding everything, all I want to do is kill.

My arms are held behind my back by both Carter and Walker. Liam and Noah drag me out of the cafeteria giving a few apologies to the ladies that service lunch every day. They don't have to deal with this. At least they don't have to clean it up. It'll be some poor sap that got detention. I need to see Avery, so she can see what she does to me.

I'm still in my own head until I realize that we're in a car driving. I don't even want to make small talk, so I don't even fucking care to ask. It's a good thing that I got away from there, I would hunt her down.

We pull up to *Pretty Girls*. It's one of the many popular strip clubs here in California. I smile; this might be actually what I need. If you put enough alcohol in a man, he would be content looking at tits and ass all day.

For the next hour, my nerves start to calm down as does my body. Five of us rarely talk, they just keep ordering me drinks getting me shit faced. This is exactly what I needed. It never crosses my mind how easy it is for us to continually get alcohol, in actuality who's gonna tell a Mancini no?

"Why don't you just fucking take her and be done with it?" Walker says, he's had a few drinks. At least I was feeling better, but not anymore.

"He likes this one," Carter growls out. We all just nod, then he continues. "All the other ones he just took to fuck them, until they were out of his system. He can't do this with Avery, he actually likes this girl. He's going to need to wine and dine her, shit like that."

It only took like two seconds for all of us to burst out laughing, except for Carter. I have never wined and dined a girl in my life. I never plan on starting.

Thankfully, everybody goes back to not saying anything and just watching the show. It's that time of day most girls come out dressed in school uniforms or as baby dolls. There is one girl that keeps grabbing my attention, she's got a nice rack and a banging body.

Liam notices me watching her as he waves her over. The man pulls out a few large bills and whispers in her ear. The girl I later find out is named Candy Apple. Candy lightly tugs on my hand and leads me to one of the fancier closed off and soundproof rooms down the hallway to the right.

I'm game. She doesn't talk which I'm grateful for, she just pushes me down in a chair and starts to do a sexy little dance, stripping off her clothes.

She nods towards my crotch letting me know her intentions. Liam must've paid a good amount for this to happen. I'm not going to bitch, especially if this girl's gonna suck me off.

My jeans and boxers are jerked down just below my hips. I'm not getting undressed in case I need to leave fast. I stroke myself as I watch her twirl on the stripper pole.

I growl out, I'm only semi-hard. All I can see is Avery's face and I remember how she felt when she was in my lap.

I start to grow in size as the girl drops to her knees in front of me, her tongue slowly coming out her mouth getting ready to lick the head of my cock.

For some reason I feel absolutely disgusted. I don't know if it's because of her or because I can't get Avery out of my damn head.

Great, she won't let me be with her, she wants nothing to do with me and at the same time she's cock blocking me.

I stand up quickly and exit the room. I want nothing to do with this girl, she's making my skin crawl, which is totally unusual. I'm a fucking warm-blooded male, the girl has a willing open mouth, my dick should be in there.

I change my seat when I get closer to the guys, leaving my back towards the dance floor. They're not even watching the girls, all four of them have their heads together probably discussing what the fuck is wrong with me.

They all see me and smile. Dumb asses, when has it ever taken me less than five minutes to get my rocks off? I have the stamina of a God.

I keep drinking as fast as they can bring it to me, as fast as I can get it to go down my throat. It doesn't take that long for me to get drunk, slurring, stumbling drunk. It also doesn't take that long for me to remind myself of Avery.

I stand up faster than I should in my state and lean against the table. It's gone on long enough. My girl needs me to fuck her. She will realize that she needs this as much as I do.

I stumble my way outside, I'm a man on a mission. I'm gonna go over to Avery's house and fuck her right now.

Out of the corner of my eye I see the guys laugh as Liam hurries up over to our waitress to pay the bill. The strippers, bartenders and waitresses are a little bit upset to see us go. It's not that busy in here right now and we were tipping like freaks. You can't have the full experience unless you tip really good.

I was gonna walk but I'm grateful that the guys help me in the car. They didn't even have to ask, they knew what my intentions were as Carter told me he'd take me over there.

The drive seems like it takes five hours, but it probably only took about ten or fifteen minutes. I can only imagine how long it would've taken if I would've walked. I chuckle to myself, they would've found me curled up on the side of the road asleep.

I exit the vehicle, shockingly without falling over, go me. I start to walk up to Avery's front door, then I realize that we're not at Avery's house, we're at Tate's. I guess it's my house right now, too, but I can't call it that until I know who the fuck owns it.

I start to bitch, but I'm so tired that nothing really comes out. I make myself go to the couch. My rooms upstairs but I don't even want to try and climb those fucking stairs. There's probably only like ten or twenty, but to me it looks like ten or twenty thousand.

"... He's pretty sloshed." I'm not even sure who's talking, but it looks like Tate is standing right by whoever it is.

"Fine, okay, I got him." Tate doesn't look incredibly happy to take care of me. With as much energy as I can muster, I hold my arms out like I'm looking for a hug. Her eyes go wide as she scoffs and heads into another room.

Each guy comes by and gives me a fist bump as they exit towards the door. I know I'm upset by something, but I can't remember, I just wish I had the energy so I could follow Tate around and give her more shit. Maybe she'll relax enough to tell me who owns this fucking house.

I fall asleep, it's not a deep sleep, it's a drunk-induced sleep. Sometimes it can be fun, but this time it's not. If Tate is here maybe Avery is here, but I don't see her anywhere.

A straw is pushed against my lips as I greedily drink the cool water. It feels so good going down my hoarse throat.

"Hey big dumb ass, you also need to swallow these pills. If you don't, you'll be more pleasant tomorrow than you normally are." I try to growl at what she says as I take the pills, but it comes out looking more like I'm constipated. God, why did they let me get so drunk?

I fall back in and out of sleep but every time I wake up Tate is sitting on the couch. Maybe she wants to make sure that I don't drop dead. That would be ridiculously hard to explain to the rest of the family.

"Please leave Avery alone, Asher." Tate says this so low that I almost don't hear her.

"I can't," I say as Tate snaps her head towards me with her eyes wide. She probably thought I was passed out and didn't hear her. "There's just something about her. I can't stop thinking about her, Tate."

Tate whispers, "oh God," right before I fall asleep. This time it sticks and I'm able to sleep the whole night. Even in my drunken state, all I can think about is Avery.

If I don't figure out what to do about this girl, I'm going to be well and truly fucked.

CHAPTER 16

AVERY

Tate's car horn pulls me out of my depression. I glance back around the house, it's dark. Even though it's morning right now none of the curtains have been opened, it feels very cold.

It feels that way because nobody's here. Arya and Garrett are in London, I believe, this time I'm not exactly sure.

Throughout my school years there's always been somebody there, always. But now there's nobody. If I was lucky, I would get to see my dad at least two times a week, he worked a lot for the Romano family business. My mom was there every day, she would always make me breakfast and wave at the front door as I left for school, usually with my driver.

I walk halfway down the steps and look back, but everything is empty. There's nobody there waving to me and saying goodbye. My parents are lost forever and they're never coming back.

As much as this all hurts, it would be kind of cool if Arya and Garrett were there right now, seeing me on my way to school making me feel like I'm not the loneliest bitch in the world.

I force myself just to get into Tate's car and not look back, I know what I'm going to see, an empty and depressing house.

I give her a tight smile when I slide in the front seat. Even though I know I shouldn't, my gaze automatically turns back to the front door. The emptiness I feel inside hopefully one day won't be like this.

I'll be the one standing at the front door waving to my family.

I glance at Tate several times on the ten-minute drive to school. Normally my friend is really happy and bubbly, but today she just looks nervous.

She's doing everything she can to avoid my gaze, she keeps biting her lips and looking out the window.

"Spill it." I'm looking directly at her now. Even my whole body is facing in her direction, with my knee up on the smooth leather seat.

She's quiet for a few seconds then she finally nods to herself. "Asher was really drunk last night, and he talked to me some."

We start to pull into the school as we both let silence hang in the air. I want her to finish before I say anything, she's definitely not done.

"He's obsessed with you Avery, like caveman obsessed." Tate takes a huge breath and finishes, "he has never had a girlfriend. That doesn't mean he can take whoever he wants without there being any repercussions." This is not going to end well at all.

"Okay, okay," I say to myself. "Having a crush is totally different than having somebody that's obsessed with you. A crush would easily leave you alone until they get the balls to actually talk to you. An obsession will not leave you alone, no matter what."

I feel like I'm going to throw up. Luca my ex was obsessed and look what that got me: dead parents, and a move across the country.

Tate grabs my hand and squeezes it. "He thought about just taking you to New York, I guess just to see if you guys can build on something there."

"What?" I asked in a shocked whisper as I snatch my hand back away. I am not going anywhere with him, I'm here to finish out my senior year and be done.

Tate tries as hard as she can to keep her face neutral, but she looks like she was cringing on top of constipation.

"You don't understand, Avery. He is a Mancini, who happens to control the Northeast, he can do whatever he wants and none of us can stop him."

"Fuck that," I mumble to myself. "Nobody tries to stop him. You all just figure he's a Mancini and in charge, so let's let him do whatever the fuck he wants." He'll understand that is not going to happen with us.

After everything I've been through in the past several months, there is no way in hell I'm going to let somebody else make choices for me. I'll go down fighting. "He'll have to take my cold fucking dead body to New York if he wants me that bad."

She gives me a small smile. She knows exactly what I'm thinking and feeling, but she's also a mafia girl, too, she just doesn't know that I am. She must have thought I would be terrified and submissively bow my head for the rest of my life and go willingly, fuck that.

"I begged him to try and court you first, let you guys fall in love naturally, not you being forced into something you don't want." Tate starts to gather her belongings before getting out of the car. "I'm so sorry, Avery, but he wouldn't budge."

I still give her another smile, hoping to relax her, letting her know I will not lose my shit. Will I succumb to my fate? *Hell no.*

If I didn't say I was freaked out I would be lying. I'm a little freaked out, but I'm not going to just lay down and take it, this is my life. I've been in this situation before, wait, scratch that, I was stuck in this situation before.

I quickly grab my stuff so I can catch up with Tate who happens to be at the front of the car slowly making her way towards the school.

I grab her hand, making her stop and look back at me. "I will never lay down and take anything, therefore I'm not going to New York." As I tell Tate these things, I mean them with every fiber of my being.

But there is no way in hell I'm going to be caught alone again with an obsessed man. I've already learned this lesson.

I do hope that's the case. I can admit that I feel something towards Asher, and I can also admit that I'm not stupid. Hopefully, he'll just realize that soon and leave me alone. He can either make my time here go by super-fast, or super slow. I really want to go back home.

Tate puts her arm through mine as we start to walk

inside. She's such a wonderful friend, the best I've ever had.

Damn it, I tell myself. I need to tell her everything, let her know exactly who I am. I plan on doing that tonight. I don't think Tate will get to upset at me, she hates this way of life probably more than I do.

———

SCHOOL TODAY WAS JUST SURREAL. EVERYONE WAS ACTING weird. Either they loved me, or they hated me.

The only ones I have a problem with are the bitch crew and their fans that follow them around, which happens to be almost half the school.

Most people just ignore me, including Asher. I haven't seen very much of him at all today, but he looked like shit from when I did see him. Tate said that he did get pretty drunk.

I can feel his eyes on me almost everywhere. I would try to shrug off the creepy feeling, but whenever I looked he was staring right at me. I'm grateful he left me alone, but I don't know what's worse: his eyes drilling holes in the back of my head or constantly having his slaves fuck with me.

Occasionally when I wasn't paying attention or just looking around, I would always find myself staring at him. For some reason, I just can't explain it. It feels like he has some magnetic pull. Like my body is wrapped in chains, and with his eyes he can pull me towards him, it's freaking creepy.

I really don't have many options on how to get him to

stay away from me. I could scour the school looking for somebody that he has some kind of interest in, and try to get them together somehow, but I'm sure that won't work.

The number one reason being, I can't even match myself up. I would absolutely suck ass as a matchmaker.

Since he's the boss of these idiots, the main man, I'm shocked that he hasn't been called back on business.

My father was always running around, and just the little bit of time I spent with my grandfather, he was busy as hell.

Way too busy to take my ass to California, but at least he did ride with me to the airport.

I groan out and shake the thoughts of my grandfather away. I wish we had more time, I'd really like to get to know him. The hours we had together were hardly enough.

I'm in my own little world floating and daydreaming as the rest of the school seems to run past me. I take my sweet time getting to my locker. I shouldn't take my time, who knows what could happen to me.

My daydream is short-lived as my shoulders are grabbed from behind and pushed into an unused classroom with an open door.

By the time I have a chance to say something or turn around and swing at the asshole that deserves it, the door is already being shut and locked as the lights flip on.

It doesn't shock me in the least when I see who pushed me in the room, Asher. His breathing is heavy, and his eyes look crazy constantly moving from each one of mine.

I gasp, I should definitely be afraid, but I'm not. I can

hear so much noise outside from the students and the teachers walking by.

"What do you want Asher?" I say trying to sound bored and annoyed. In reality though my heart is beating fast, even though there are people right outside. I'm starting to get nervous.

"You," he spits out as he pushes himself into my body, slowly making us back up against the wall next to the door.

His hands grip my wrists as he pushes them both up, parallel to both sides of my head.

He doesn't move or say anything, he just keeps looking at me, like maybe he can see into my soul and figure me out.

I study his face as much as he did mine. Looking between both of his eyes and his nose that looks like it's been broken multiple times. I can't forget about his kissable lips. God his lips looks so soft. Before I realize, I find myself leaning into him. I stop myself instantly, I know that it probably wasn't noticeable because I barely moved in his direction.

I was wrong, though. It seems nothing gets by him as he smirks, knowing exactly what I was doing.

I push him trying to get some space so I can breathe and think, he pushes back just as hard, pushing his body into mine. There's not one place that doesn't feel hard to my softness, this man is fucking built.

"I want you Avery," he growls as his hands move my wrists above my head. He transfers one hand into another, not letting me move.

He lets his fingers explore everywhere, over the side of

my face, over my lips. On instinct I moan causing my lips to open, but I'm quick to press them tight together again.

He goes really slow as his finger travels over my collarbone and down in between my breasts. I decided to wear a tight tank top with a pair of my old favorite leggings today. I bite my lip in frustration as I realize I should've wore jeans and a chastity belt.

He leans his head down into the curve of my neck and in inhales. "Let me just fuck you out of my system, Avery. Then we can both be done with this."

I want to ask him how we're both involved in this, but I shut my mouth. Heat is building at my core and I have goosebumps all over my body. Maybe if I let him fuck me this will all be done.

He can see me going through my options, trying to figure out what to do. His smile gets bigger the longer I'm competing with myself.

It's been awhile and honestly, Luca sucked in bed. The only time I had sex was when he took my virginity, so I imagine that it was just horrible because of him. For some reason I don't think Asher would make it so bad.

I wonder if he thinks that I'm contemplating opening my legs for him right here in the fucking school classroom. I glance around real fast to see where we are, and if we are in a school classroom. *We are.*

He starts to gyrate his hips managing to get in between my legs, showing me how much he really wants me. I won't be shocked if this is one of those cases where if he doesn't come, he's going to be forever having trouble with a huge case of blue balls.

A moan accidentally slips out when he hits the perfect

spot. My eyes widen, I can't believe I did that. Asher's eyes sparkle with laughter, he knows exactly what he's doing to me.

I'm quickly yanked from the wall, flipped around, and slammed down onto what must be the desk in the front of the classroom. I can't turn around and see what's going on behind me, since I'm on my stomach. He is keeping my wrists pinned together on my lower back with one of his hands.

Now I'm starting to get scared, this isn't happening. "No, no, no," I plead with Asher, but he's not listening, his breathing is coming in heavy pants and he's got a crazy look in his eyes. It hurts to turn around to try to look at him with how hard he's pressing me down. I need him to see me. I need him to see that I don't want this right now, and that I'm actually scared.

Asher moves fast, pulling down my leggings along with my thong. I can feel the chilly air hit my core. The tears start to pool in my eyes. I don't want to go through this again.

I know I'm shaking so badly as Asher's hand comes up and starts to rub my back and my arms. "Relax baby, your body wants this just as much as I do. Just think, we could fuck each other out of our systems and be done with this."

I shake my head no. "Not like this, please." I don't know if he pretends like he doesn't hear me or if he just doesn't care.

One of his legs steps in between mine as he uses his index and middle finger to part my lips. A finger slowly works its way up from my ass to my clit.

Before I realized anything is happening, he's pushing

into me with his finger. Oh God, I say to myself as my body shivers. Even though I don't want this, I have to admit this feels freaking fantastic. I don't know if he's a whiz with what he's doing or what.

I imagine all the assholes out in the world that want to take a girl against her will, will think that their magic dick and their magic fingers will do everything to change her mind, but it doesn't.

I don't know if my situation is different or maybe because I just connect with him on a physical basis. Even though my body is screaming yes, the rest of me screaming no. It's too soon after what happened before.

I can hear the zipper on Asher's jeans go down.

Hell no, I say to myself as I shake my head. There is no way in hell this is going to happen. The next time I have sex with a guy, it's going to be on my terms and not his. I realize that I need to find a guy that's not in the mafia, some sweet man that probably doesn't exist.

They don't exist because they're boring.

I take a deep breath and scream as loud as I can, fuck him if he thinks this is going to happen.

He snaps out, "fuck," and then quickly covers my mouth with one of his hands. His body is leaning over me now. Thankfully, he didn't get his jeans down, he could have easily slipped inside me.

"Avery, shut the fuck up," he snaps at me in my ear. I'm still just screaming through the palm that's covering my mouth.

The door of the classroom starts pounding, most likely from teachers and not students.

"Open up." That voice sounds like the Dean.

"This is not funny anymore, open the door now." I don't recognize that voice, but I could tell it's a woman, probably one of the other teachers.

"Call security," I hear the Dean snap out.

"Avery, is that you? Asher, you better not have my friend in there, you fucking asshole."

Asher curses realizing this isn't going to happen, especially now that Tate is here, thank God.

He lets go of me and I quickly pull back up my leggings as he dresses himself.

I make my way through the door which is only a few feet away as Asher grabs me. "This is going to happen one way or another Avery."

I shake my head and before I even get a word out he continues, "I can't get you out of my fucking head. We will either happen or you will have one hell of a time trying to survive school." He runs a hand down his face, obviously annoyed with me and probably those still beating on the door trying to get in.

"One way or another you belong to me. Until you realize that, your life is going to be fucking miserable."

Asher goes to stomp out of the room, but I stop him. "This isn't how you treat somebody you like. I can only imagine how you treat somebody that you love." Asher just stares at me, maybe in shock that I spoke up or maybe he's actually getting what I said.

"Stay the fuck away from me Asher," I move my finger between us multiple times. "We will never fucking happen." I go out the door slamming it behind me.

"Avery Stone, are you okay?" I keep getting a bunch of calls out from different teachers and the Dean wanting to make sure I'm okay. I ignore all of them. I grab Tate by the arm as we hurry down the hall.

For some reason I feel I will always keep kicking myself in the ass for this when I look back. Asher comes out and looks around, both ways down the hall until he spots me. His eyes darken as I flip him off.

I can see the threat in his eyes alone. I know this isn't over, but fuck him, he still doesn't know who I am.

His determined and deadly stare don't have as much impact on me as the fact that all the teachers and the dean put their heads down and walked away when Asher came out.

This is some crazy fucking world we live in.

CHAPTER 17

ASHER

I barely paid attention to the ride home from school. I know I've been pacing the foyer for at least twenty minutes.

My hands keep fisting at my side, but I try to rein it in. I've already punched the wall by the door twice. I'll make sure I have it fixed very soon, so I don't have to listen to Tate bitching any more than she already does.

I honestly wish there was somebody here that I hated. Maybe one of the Romano's, just so I can take my aggression out on them. I need to fight or fuck, that's really going to be the only thing that calms my ass down.

This time I scream as I punch a huge ass hole in the front door. At least it's on the inside so nobody will notice.

"Fuck!" That one hurts like a bitch. My knuckles are split open and bleeding.

My anger has only temporarily subsided. It's still

boiling through my blood. I feel like I could turn into a fucking werewolf right now.

I almost fucked Avery in a classroom when she was telling me 'no'. I've never taken a woman against her will, and I don't want to start now.

My father used to tell me, sometimes women need help on deciding. If their body's all for it, then all they need is a little extra push.

Even though Avery didn't want it, maybe she was scared, her body was crying for it. When I slid my fingers inside of her that girl was wetter than just getting out of the bathtub.

I know my dad was an idiot, he basically tried to talk his way out of forcing a woman to have sex with him.

"She needs to leave," I say out loud as I walk over to the bar setup, right by the dining room. This place is nice, but it's not what I'm used to. I could probably fit at least five of these houses in the Mancini compound.

Three drinks and twenty minutes later, I start to calm down. I should just go out and find myself somebody to fuck. I could call Paisley or one of her stupid bitch friends. They won't be able to help, Avery is the only one that could take all this shit away.

But what if I'm wrong?

What if I fuck this girl seven ways to Sunday and nothing's changed? It's possible I could even become more obsessed with her.

She has to go, Avery Stone needs to leave the fucking state.

I sigh as I plop down on a leather couch, setting my drink and the bottle on the coffee table. I know exactly what she'll say before I ask her, Avery is very headstrong. She would either tell me to fuck off or laugh in my face.

There's no other solution. I can't get her under me, so I need to get her as far away from me as possible. I'm the fucking boss of the Mancini family. I can't lose control, lives could be lost, mistakes made. This can never happen again.

The door opens as an annoyed Tate comes in followed by my four best friends. Even though Liam works for me, I still consider him one of my closest confidants besides Doppler.

The fucker followed me across the country just so he wouldn't have to stay in New York. At least he still needed to finish high school.

Carter Beckett is also one of the friends of the family, he just wanted to get away from the insanity that is New York and decided to enroll in school.

The fucker didn't even ask his parents, he just went where he wanted to. His parents are scary as shit. Carter is a whole new world unto himself. If I was a normal man, I would stay the fuck away from him, but since I'm not, and I'm technically his boss, I do whatever I can to piss him off.

Tate heads for the kitchen, as all the guys drop their asses on the living room couch and turn on the TV.

I grab four more glasses and another bottle of whiskey, at least Tate has the good shit.

I wait a few minutes until they're all comfortable. "Avery Stone means nothing to me, she is hereby ousted."

A few eyebrows raise and look in my direction, most likely from just being shocked by what I've said. I've never in my entire life ousted somebody from school or from the family. Since I'm doing this now, they must know that I'm serious.

"What!" Tate screams from the kitchen as she runs into the living room sliding to a stop. Her face is red and angry. I'm glad that she actually doesn't have a knife in her hands, the girl looks pissed. "You leave Avery the fuck alone. She's done nothing to you. You don't know what kind of hell she's had to go through."

Tate squeezes her eyes shut at the last comment. She doesn't know what's happened to Avery, either. Why would she say something like that? She might not know what happened, but she can tell that something has. Interesting.

"What the fuck is wrong with you?" Tate screams. Thankfully, all she had in her hands was a dish rag that she threw at me and not a ceramic plate.

I jump to my feet and storm towards her, she knows this shit ain't going to work.

Carter grabs her from behind and holds her close to his body as I step right in front of her. "This is none of your fucking concern Tate, if you have a problem with it, I can always get a hold of Armani."

The fear in her eyes is very noticeable, even the stupidest idiot in the world would be able to tell by looking at her face. My niece is scared shitless of her brothers, and for good reason. If they got a hold of her right now, they'd beat the shit out of her as restitution for leaving and trying to find another life away from her own.

"Keep your nose in your own fucking business, Tate.

Or I'll make a fucking phone call." I spit the last part out at her.

Tate nods frantically, there is nothing scarier to that girl than her brothers. At this point in time with what she did, I wouldn't even be shocked if they killed her, well, at least Armani. Gino would do everything in his power to fight for her and protect her.

"You're a fucking asshole Asher, even if she did like you, you don't deserve her you son of a bitch!" Tate screams as she runs by us all back up to her room.

In all honesty I feel a little guilty for doing that. I never want her brothers to get a hold of her, but that will happen one day, and she'll just have to deal with it. Hopefully, I can at least ease the situation. My nephew's will not go against me but keeping up with family protocol I will have to let them get revenge and make her show respect somehow.

I wish I didn't have to. My humanity is screaming at the top of my head not to let it happen. When Tate gets a bug up her ass again, who's to say she won't leave? When they get ahold of her, I can guarantee you she won't leave again unless she's got a death wish.

Football's on TV and the guys are getting ready for the start of the new season. Even though we've been training for a while, it'd be nice to start playing for real.

"You guys need to get the word out about Avery Stone." I don't say anything else, we all just relax and watch the game. This is what I needed to do to calm my ass down, well that and a bottle of whiskey.

"Are you sure about this Asher?" Noah looks at me, he's the nicest one of us all.

"Yep, if she doesn't leave I don't know what I'll do. I might end up killing her." As I say the last part they all snap their gazes towards me, they probably weren't expecting that.

Carter burst out laughing, which is very unusual for him. He's the quiet one of us all, and hates to talk, he never speaks unless spoken to and that's only if he cares to reply.

I just sit there and watch him for a couple minutes. Walker and Noah bust out laughing, too, but Liam's face remains neutral and so does mine.

"Oh my God," Carter manages to say between his laughing fits. "You are so pussy-whipped. I've never seen this." Carter continues to laugh. Unfortunately for me so does Walker and Noah.

Liam's face is a little red and he has a twinkle in his eye. I know he wants to let go, but he can't, he's my right-hand man.

"Fucker," I snarl as I leave the living room and head up to my room. Even though I look angry, a slight smirk appears on my face. Maybe I am pussy whipped.

THE CAFETERIA IS WHERE IT'S SUPPOSED TO START. I'VE BEEN waiting all morning, I'm not exactly fond of watching what they do to Avery, but I'm very curious how she handles it. I'm early today, the teacher is finishing up the lesson, I wanted to be here. I got my lunch and am positioned in my seat. I'm all comfortable and waiting for the action to begin.

After I went to bed, I sent the guys a group message. Even though Avery is ousted she's still off limits, no one can touch her. Carter sent me back an emoji, as the rest of the group gave me a thumbs up.

Now it's time for the show as the cafeteria starts to fill up. I'm going to let all these idiots do my bidding. This is the part of my life that actually makes me happy.

In the beginning when I turned seventeen, I became a made man. When I turned nineteen, I took over everything. My father was killed during a negotiation talk, he was a dumb ass, he stupidly trusted everyone.

Am I upset that he's gone, fuck no, but I'm not happy, either. I wasn't expecting to deal with this shit for at least twenty to thirty more years.

Students that walk into the cafeteria give me knowing smirks, well, only those that are helping. God, everyone must be so fucking bored, if this is what they have to look forward to, but then I can't really say anything as I'm comfortably seated upon my throne waiting for the action to happen.

Apparently, it's not going to take a long time, either, as Tate and Avery make their way into the cafeteria and stand in line.

Both of the girls stand there and take rude insults, even napkins and other gross objects thrown in their direction. For a second, I thought Tate and Avery were going to get into a fight with a few of the cheerleaders that hang out with Paisley and her group.

Nothing happened though. I know I told them they couldn't touch her, but everybody likes a good fight every now and then.

I kind of wish Avery had different friends. The only real reason they're not touching Tate is because she's a Mancini. If they only knew right now, at this point in time, I honestly don't give a shit.

Tate knows the hold that Avery has over me. I know she's trying to get her friend to stay, not just because they're good friends, but because if Avery leaves, I really have no reason to be here anymore, and then neither will Tate.

I haven't decided what I'm going to do when she finally does relent and leaves. I do like the quiet and simplicity of being here instead of in New York, but it makes things harder, especially with work being so far away.

For the next twenty minutes my guys and I watch as people casually pass by Avery's table. Something always happens, whether it's throwing food or calling out names.

A few of the football players that haven't even made it to varsity yet, decide to sit at their table.

I'm not moving, I want to see how things are going. I don't like them sitting so close to Avery, a little too close for my liking.

Liam must be able to tell the shift in me as I start to stand up. He grabs my arm and shakes his head.

"Relax man, see how this plays out. If you run every time somebody touches her, everyone's going to think she's off limits. Fuck, they won't even bother messing with her anymore. They don't want to get their asses kicked." I nod, the fucker's right.

I do my best to avoid looking in that direction, at least until those jocks move. I'm starving so I decide to eat my already cold lunch, five minutes later I look back up and they're still sitting there.

Two of the jocks have their arms around both of the girls. I instantly stand up only to be dragged back down by Walker and Liam.

Most of the cafeteria watches as voices are raised over at Avery's table. They're not liking being touched at all.

Those girls simultaneously stand up and dump their trays all over the two deserving assholes.

The one right by Tate decides to grab her ass as she was standing up. "Dumb fucker!" I can hear her yell out right before her tray is smashed over his head. He goes still as his body rolls out of the chair and onto the floor.

The whole cafeteria blows up in laughter while both of the girls quickly make their way outside.

The guy that got hit with the tray is up on his feet with a face redder than anything I've ever seen. He's trying to go after the girls as his friend physically has to stop him and drag his weak ass back to their normal table.

All of us chuckle. "It could have gone a lot better, but that was pretty entertaining to watch." I say as their eyes are still focused on Avery's table.

I'm feeling pretty elated, my plan is going to work perfectly. After everything, these people did to Avery, she'll be gone tonight. I thought I would feel a lot better by that, but for some reason I don't. Not seeing her anymore creates an emptiness inside of me.

I AM IN FUCKING HEAVEN, AFTER ALL THIS TIME, I CRAWL over Avery's naked body spread out on my bed. I'm about to slam inside of my girl when the door jerks open.

The wooden door to my room bounces off the inside wall as the lights go on. I open my eyes and sit straight up, reaching for the hand-gun on my nightstand.

"You son of a bitch!" Tate screams as she throws the shoe she just took off her foot at my head.

I swat it away and then groan out, "fuck." I run my hands over my face. She has fucking impeccable timing. I was finally going to sink into Avery until fucking Tate decides to interrupt me. Even though it was only a dream, it felt fucking real.

"You don't know anything about Avery, you don't know what she's been through, you don't know where she's come from, none of us do. So how fucking dare you sick your guys on her because she doesn't want you."

Damn it, I really don't have time for this. I just want to roll back over and go back to bed. But if I do, Tate won't leave me alone, it's better that I just let her get all the shit off her chest.

"Do you have any idea what happened to her today? Sexual assault, and you are also responsible."

That snaps my head up to attention, I don't know what went on in the classroom with her and Avery.

"You didn't know about that? I'm shocked seeing how you control all the little puppets in this school to do your bidding."

Tate looks like she's about ready to jump me and try to beat the shit out of me.

Luckily, she starts to pace in front of the bed instead.

"Besides all the name calling, the food throwing, stealing her clothes from the locker room. Oh, and my favorite," she turns to look at me, "is when they decided during this, maybe it was English, to see how many times they could physically grab her. I'm not just talking about her legs or arms. I'm talking about how each of them would get a point for grabbing her boobs."

"What!" I yell out as I jump up. I know I'm in my boxers, but freaking Tate is like a sister to me, she is my niece. I don't even think it would faze her if she saw me naked, it might just gross her out.

"Oh yeah, they successfully managed to grab her several times before she started fighting back." Tate sighs and takes a seat on the edge of the bed. I start to pace. "You're a fucking idiot Asher. I don't understand how you could be so high up the ladder, but so fucking stupid!" She yells out the last word and slams the door on her way out.

"Fuck!" I was not expecting that. I left specific instructions that nobody touches her.

Me: find out the names of the assholes that touched Avery in last period.

Liam: got it boss.

I am not backing down with what I'm doing, these fucking idiots need to do as I say, and definitely not touch what's mine. I almost choke on that last word. I cannot physically claim her if I'm trying to banish her.

I get that thought straight the fuck out of my head. There is no way I'm going down this road, I've already decided, she's gone. What I will do is beat the shit out of those that defy my direct orders.

They decided to touch her when I said she was off

limits. They were doing it more for themselves instead of for me. We'll see how they feel tomorrow, after I beat the fuck out of them.

Under no circumstances does this change anything. I still will do everything in my power to push her away, even if it makes her hate me.

By the time everything is said and done. I'm fairly sure this girl will hate me.

CHAPTER 18

AVERY

When the doorbell rings instead of the honk letting me know that Tate's here, I stop in my tracks a little weirded out.

Not once since Tate's been picking me up for school has she ever come up and rang the doorbell.

Don't get me wrong, it's not like she's afraid to come in the house, but normally when she does, she just bursts right in.

It takes me a second to realize it and then when I do I burst out laughing, Asher thinks the same as all the other idiots at the school, that I'm going to curl up in a ball and cry myself out of the state.

Too bad these people have no idea what I've been through. Shit, this bullying thing is child's play.

If you really want to show somebody how much you hate them or how much they're affecting you, go ahead and kill their parents and try to burn them alive. That's where you get the most attention.

I shudder at that as my eyes gloss over, it was a little harsh but it's the truth. I take a deep breath as I walk towards the door. It takes more than what they've done to me for me to leave. Asher must think I'm a pussy and am going to run home.

I'm not affected, nor will I ever be by the rich brats at the school, but I am affected by the loss of my family, the only way to really get through that is with time. I haven't had that much time, it hasn't even been six months yet.

Most people get a chance to grieve when bad shit happens to them, not me. No, I get to continue running for my life because the person that wanted to burn me originally didn't fulfill his destiny. So now I get to stay hidden as well as I can.

The thing that cracks me up the most is these little losers with almost no life experience trying to dictate the way other people live, they know nothing about.

Of course, I would love to scream, "hit me with your best shot." I've been through more than having harsh words thrown at me or even a few used dirty napkins heading in my direction.

The guys that try to cop a feel, I don't even think they've ever felt one before. They were more shocked than I was when they made contact.

Fucking idiotic virgins. What these damn rich kids need in the school is some life experience. Don't get me wrong there's several of us, like me, Asher, most likely Liam, and I have a feeling even Carter. That boy keeps to himself, but there's just some underlying darkness inside of him that I can't pinpoint. It's like Asher let his darkness run straight through him.

I take a deep breath getting ready to open the door. I don't want my good mood to be spoiled today.

If I didn't have the life I did, I would imagine I would be in a corner of this house crying my eyes out until somebody came home and told me it was going to be all right.

I look around the house again realizing that that's not going to be an option for me.

More than anything I want to be able to ask Garrett and Arya to stay home for a while. Shit, maybe if I offer to help them with some work, I don't know exactly what I can do, but you never know, it might free up enough time so that they can just hang out at the house.

I imagine they'd be incredibly bored, the house is already immaculately clean. There is no honey-do list that needs done. I wonder if they've ever just sat in front of a TV and binge watched a show, something that relaxes them. My mind's made up, I'm going to try to get them to stay home for a week. Shit, I'd even take a weekend.

I open the front door to a very solemn looking Tate. She doesn't even look like she normally does, her eyes are puffy, and her hair is just straight and boring. That girl's always doing something with it. Even her uniform is normal and bland today. She's one of those that has a few buttons open at the top and the skirt pulled up a couple inches, none of that's done today. She either got dressed in a hurry or she just didn't care.

Take looks me over, noticing my school uniform. Her eyes widen, she didn't expect me to be here. Damn girl even texted me probably twenty times seeing if I was going to leave and every single time I told her no.

"I told you I wasn't leaving. You need to quit worrying about me so much. I have been through much worse than this." I start to feel guilty again. I need to just tell her everything that happened to me, I don't want any more secrets between us. I know she's got a doozy of her own, like who owns that house she's living in.

She smiles as she crushes me in a hug. "I just knew. I had this feeling all night that when I got over here you would be gone, that you wouldn't want to deal with them anymore."

I chuckle. "Believe me I don't want to deal with them anymore, but what they're doing is just a game." I really wanted to say, if they only knew what happened to me but then of course Tate would want to know what happened to me right now, too. I'm not ready for that especially standing in my house right before school. "Let's go, I don't want to be late." That would give them more shit to try to mess with me on.

She nods as we make our way to her car. Silence followed us all the way to school. Normally I like to look out the window, California is so different than the East Coast. The palm trees and sunny days are nice, but not today. Maybe the assholes at school are getting to me, but in a different way. I'm feeling melancholy missing everyone, especially my mom.

The atmosphere at the school is ten times different than it was after the bullying. These people actually thought I would leave.

I'm trying to make myself out to be a badass, but this is fucking ridiculous. Bullying wasn't even that bad. Yeah, I got groped and shit thrown at me, plus some nasty names, but damn it, that was it.

A couple of the jocks that felt me up are standing at the edge of the parking lot, not too far from the front doors. I can see the shock written on their faces as soon as they see me. When the shock dissipates their eyebrows raise up, one of the idiots starts to slowly thrust his hips in my direction.

I burst out laughing, I can't hold it in anymore. These jocks actually think I'm back because of their extensive knowledge on feeling me up.

By the time we walk through the front door Tate and I are crying from laughing so hard. It's good for the body and the soul to let loose and enjoy your surroundings, no matter how much everything sucks.

I couldn't even prepare myself for what happens next. So far, I would consider this to be the highlight of my freaking school year. It's one of those little memories you like to pocket and keep for later especially when you need a good laugh.

Tate and I walk in through the main entrance expecting the worst, shocked stares from the other students is what we got.

What we weren't expecting was for Asher and his crew along with the bitch crew at the end of the hallway to be staring at us. Of course, Paisley was wrapped all over him, that doesn't shock me at all, but the boy's magnificent godlike jaw fully opened, I swear that bitch hit the floor and snapped right back up. All the students here in California tan like it's a religion, except for me, I'm so white and pasty.

Asher has a gorgeous tan, too, but the moment he saw me his skin went white. Maybe I should pull him aside and remind him as the head of the Mancini family he shouldn't show weakness, he is showing it tenfold right now.

With his mouth hanging open and his discolored skin, his eyes showed fear. Luckily for him it only took him a few seconds to realize what he was doing. His mouth quickly snapped shut and his skin started turning red.

Tate and I are in tears, not because we're scared, because we're laughing so hard. She sees the exact same thing I do. I know we need to cut it out. We may be in a private school and they do offer some form of protection for their students, but this still is a Mancini.

I give him a wink through all the tears. I've no idea how I managed to do that. Tate yanks on my arm, dragging us both to our locker. Thankfully, Asher's not standing by his, he's down there with everybody else. If he thinks that I left maybe he'll change lockers and go back down there where he belongs, I know that's just hopeful thinking.

The morning plays out the same as every other morning, except this time I don't look for it. I don't pay attention who comes in the classrooms and I don't acknowledge whatever they do to get a reaction out of me.

At lunch time Tate's running late, so she said she'll meet me in the cafeteria. She even did an extensive text message about me waiting outside her classroom, so I don't have to face this alone, blah blah blah.

I decided I needed to face this alone, let everybody see

me by myself, maybe this will show them that they can't get to me. I'm not stupid enough to realize they won't up their game. That's something I would do if I was trying to get rid of somebody, but these people are just Asher's little minions that will do whatever he wants. I don't even think they know the reality of why they're doing it. I don't even think they care as long as they can get on his good side.

I sit down in our normal spot with my cheeseburger and fries, so good. Mondays are usually the one day I'm happy to be in the lunchroom just because of the cheeseburgers.

I knew my cherished peace and quiet wouldn't last long. After eating for several minutes, I hear a hush go over the room. I'm not dumb enough to not know what's going on.

There's really no reason to focus on Asher since him and his whole group of people are currently heading my way. Fuck, maybe I should have waited for Tate, but this has to be done and I have to get through it.

Even as Asher steps in front of my table, I continue to eat nonchalantly not paying attention.

"You really shouldn't eat that," Paisley says as she looks at my food and then my body. The dumb bitch is trying to make a fat joke, I'm pretty much stick thin and slightly curvy is a long way from that.

"Are they out of blood bags today?" If she had fangs they would have come out now. She doesn't like the vampire jokes everybody gives her. Her dumb ass doesn't realize they can also be taken as a compliment. Gorgeous, thin, and curvy just like all the vampires I've ever read, plus the fact that I don't think any of us have seen her eat.

She tries to come at me, but Asher grips his hold around her waist not letting her move. "Not now Paisley."

Some of the students have moved in towards us to listen, as Asher sits down at the table in front of me with his minions flanking him at every fucking angle available.

"Listen Avery, I can't do this with you anymore." I'm stuck here while I eat, but I'm not stupid. By the way his eyes are sparkling, he's up to something. "I'm flattered that you came to the school for me, but I just don't want to be with you anymore. I don't always want to fuck you in the ass." He gives me a small smile that only I can see. "You're the first woman that I've ever been with that's been too loose, it's probably because of all the guys that you were with. Don't get me wrong, I'm glad your ass is still tight so that I can get off, but your vag is looser than a two-dollar hooker."

I barely heard the last part before the whole cafeteria exploded in thunderous laughter. All I want is to finish my meal in privacy and not deal with any of these idiots.

"Original." If I said this didn't bother me some I would be lying. Of course, it hurts when everybody is ganging up on you, but it's all words. That's all it will ever be. I'll never let them know everything I've experienced. They can keep having their fun, unfortunately at my expense.

I put my head down as the tears start to fill up my eyes. It's not necessarily what he said, it feels like the whole cafeteria's against me. I know it'd be better if Tate was here, but I can't get my hopes up for that, either.

Just as I thought of Tate, Asher is pushed to the side.

"Get the fuck away from her Asher, or we can really start spilling stories." Tate isn't willing to back down.

To say I was surprised when Asher does back down would be an understatement, I was freaking shocked. He gives me a wink before him, and all the other dumb asses start to go back to their area. Most of the school is still laughing and several of the kids are crying. Well at least I can make everybody else's day brighter.

Hopefully now I can eat in peace. Since I looked like I was doing okay Tate runs over and grabs her plate of food, and we both eat in wonderful silence. She knows I don't like to talk about this that much, neither one of us are in the mood for talking.

THE NEXT WEEK ISN'T EVEN ANY DIFFERENT FROM THE LAST. Some of the idiots have stepped up their game, more harder things are thrown. Plus, I'm getting at least several offers a day about getting it in the ass. The most depressing part of it is, I believe that everybody that made offers to me actually wanted to fuck me in the ass.

Thankfully, nobody's touched me, and I have a good feeling that's from Asher's orders. As long as they don't move on to ceramic or glass ashtrays or coffee mugs, whatever they throw at me, I should be fine.

I do know if things don't change soon, this year is going to drag on. That's one thing that I'm definitely not looking forward to.

Since everyone seems to know me, and how much the head of the Mancini family hates my existence, I seriously doubt if I'm going to be asked out on date, or even go to prom.

That makes my eyes fill up with tears again, my mother should be helping me prepare for prom and get ready.

What the hell is wrong with me? I've cried more in this small amount of time I've been at this school, than in my whole life.

Damn it, I can't think about this now. I've got to focus on me and my other shit. It's harder now just getting through the day.

I'M ONLY ABLE TO SEE TATE WHEN SHE PICKS ME UP AND during the school day. I'm sure asshat has some kind of hold over her, where she can't even leave the house. It's been this way for the last week, at least it's Friday.

I want to tell Tate everything, but I didn't want to do it at school. That's all I need is for somebody else to hear. At least her guards didn't take her cell phone away from her.

Friday and I'm at home and bored again, by myself as always. I sound like a bad country song about poor little me and how much my life sucks. I need to find something to keep me occupied. I thought about going and seeing if they need help at the diner just on the weekends. I don't need to work at all, I only do it just to meet people and get out of my boredom. The Stones are supposed to take care of any need I have.

Getting rides every day, I think I might actually ask for a car. Maybe if I did get a job at the diner I can make the monthly payment myself and there would be no problem.

Garrett is more of the financial whiz, he's tried talking to me a couple times about my inheritance, but right now I don't want anything to do with it. I would just prefer him, and Grandpa take care of it, at least till I can get through my grief. I want to be able to think about my parents without bursting out in tears.

All day at school I thought about telling Tate, I finally decided even if I've got to do it over the phone my best friend deserves to know.

"Hello," I pulled out my phone and called Tate before I had a chance to reconsider. The obvious place to talk to her is in person, but that can't happen right now. I can see her finding out some other time, then thinking of me as the devil in disguise. She would probably think that I was sent here by my family, like I'm some lethal killer, to take out all of the Mancini's.

I laugh. "Sorry about that, I was just thinking of something." I take a deep breath; it's now or never. "I wanted to tell you who I am, and where I come from."

"Okay, you do have this aura of surprise. It's like you're this hidden killer that nobody knows about."

I smile but it doesn't reach my eyes, this is exactly what I was afraid of but there's no stopping now. Right as I'm ready to tell her my full name someone knocks on the front door. They don't knock, they pound, like it's the freaking police department. "Who the fuck is that?" I say to myself as I start to walk towards the stairs. "Tate, you mind if I call you back. Somebody's at the door?"

"That's fine babe, I'm just sitting here bored off my ass,

but you hardly ever get visitors, so call me right back." A much lower person would take that comment as offensive, but I know she's right.

"I will," I say as I hang up the phone and make my way down towards the front door. It's only eight at night, so it's not too late or too early, but the problem is nobody comes over, ever.

I take a deep breath as I yank open the door. The element of surprise works both ways.

For several seconds I'm stunned, my mouth drops all the way open. "Grandpa?" This must have been what Asher felt like when he saw me in the cafeteria.

CHAPTER 19

Avery

"Oh my God you're here," I cry as I throw my arms around him.

At first my grandfather stiffens, then he relaxes and melts right into me. I hug him with everything I got, he doesn't realize how much I needed this today, how much I needed somebody who is family to be around me.

"Avery," a sob breaks through as my grandfather ushers me back into the house closing the door behind us. Shit, I just realized that we were out in the open. My grandfather is a myth, some people still think he's dead and for those that don't, they want to kill him.

I follow my grandfather in as he walks straight over to the Stone's bar. He takes several sips before he even turns around to look at me, this can't be good.

I follow him over to the couch and grab a bottle of water on my way. For some reason I think that we both need to have a drink, and I really don't want to grab a glass of whiskey in front of him. Who knows which way he'll go, he'll either put on the parental hat, or not care and give me a smile for boozing it up with him.

I'm not chancing it though, I don't want to piss him off. I actually wish he had luggage and was going to stay, but that would be extremely dangerous for both of us. I curse myself for not looking around outside. I wonder how many guards he has with him. Shit, my grandpa's probably a bad ass and there ain't nobody here with him. He turns into *Jet Lee* and can handle everything by himself.

"Why are you here?" I ask after waiting several minutes with no communication. I have at least a thousand questions I would love to ask him, but those are reserved for another time. A time that's not on the verge of war, a time where we're sitting down for a family meal. It would be awesome if Arya and Garrett were here, too.

"I wanted to check in on you," he says taking another huge pull of his drink. "I know that Arya and Garrett aren't here that much. After what happened to you," he looks at me with tears in his eyes, "with what happened to your parents and everything else you might be going through. I just needed to make sure you're okay."

I don't know what it is, maybe my period's getting ready to start, but the tears kind of free flow down my cheeks. I don't bother wiping them. There's really no reason, it'll keep happening.

"We're still unable to get a location on Luca, his family isn't even offering anything up. We do have someone within the ranks of the Delano's, but they haven't seen or heard anything," my grandfather says as he finishes off his glass. "They're being extra careful, they know that we're looking for him. Only a few people know his where-abouts. I seriously doubt he's even in Chicago." I take a deep breath, I know exactly what he's going to say. "He's here. There's no other place for him to be, plus the fact he has been spotted in California down by San Diego."

Luca Delano was the biggest mistake of my life. I wish with every fiber of my being that I could go back and smack myself silly before I accepted a date with him.

Grandpa tells me a little bit about what's been going down on the East Coast, but not that much. We both know that I'm not really in this life. Yes, I know all about it, but I'm not familiar with the inner dealings. That's the way I like it. I can't even imagine what this man has gone through.

It saddens my heart because we don't know each other well enough to talk about other stuff. The only way that we know each other is because my parents died, and he was there to help.

"So, my sweet Avery, how have things been going for you?" There's no time like the present, I guess, to finally ask him.

"There is something I wanted to talk to you about. I have made a friend and I'm getting a ride every day to school, but I was wondering if there is any way I can borrow enough money for a down payment for a car. I have a job at the diner if I want it, that's where I worked this summer. I could make the monthly car payments myself." I take in a deep breath, I got everything I wanted to say to him out in one breath.

My grandfather goes to talk but I hold up my hand. "I'm really good financially and I know this is a big thing to ask for help, but I promise I'll be able to take care of every payment. If you want, before I get a car, I can make sure I have several months saved up for payments and insurance. I just don't know what else..."

My grandfather's laughing is what causes me to shut my mouth. Not just a little chuckle, a full out roaring belly laugh that lasts at least five-minutes, but it was most likely only seconds.

He pulls out what looks to be a black card from his back pocket and slides it across the coffee table towards me. "This is a small part of your inheritance. The rest you'll get when you graduate high school. There is more than enough to get any car you want."

And cue the fucking tears. "I can't believe this, thank you," I say between sobs.

My grandfather lays his hand over mine that's still hovering over the credit card. Not just any credit card, a black American Express credit card. If this is a small part of my inheritance, I can only imagine what the whole thing is.

"That's part of the reason I wanted to come, Arya and Garrett tell me you don't ask for anything." My grandfather laughs as he gets up and walks over to the bar. "Garrett was a little bit irritated that you even got a job and started buying groceries." My grandfather's full out laughing hunched over next to the bar with his hands on his knees while I'm sitting here crying. I guess we've got a different view of things.

It takes several minutes for both of us to calm down and regain our breath.

"You need to be careful Avery, I hired several guards

for you. Nobody will infringe on your privacy, everybody will be outside, but I want to give you several different numbers in case of an emergency. If something does happen all you need to do is scream and you'll have twenty to thirty men rush in."

I'm shocked to learn how many guards I have. "Don't get me wrong, you still need to stay vigilant and careful. Things are starting to change with the Mancini's, and I don't think it's that little incident that happened anymore. I fully believe that they're going to try to take the whole East Coast." He shakes his head slumping into the seat next to me. "The smartest thing would be to get you the fuck out of here, and away from all this, but it's not the safest, not with Luca on the loose." He turns and looks at me making sure I understand everything he's talking about. "Avoid the Mancini's like they're the plague, it's the only thing that's going to keep you safe. Hopefully all this shit will be over as fast as it started."

Now is the perfect moment I should tell him I'm not alone in this. I should tell my grandfather how I'm best friends with the niece of Asher Mancini, let's not forget I would also tell the wise old man what Asher has been doing to me, what the whole school has been doing. My leaving the school will probably get me killed faster than staying here. Asher does talk a lot of a shit, but he doesn't just want to end me, he wants to fuck me.

"I will. I'll be as careful as I can Grandpa." I smile as I say the last part. I will be as careful as I can but I'm not going to lay around and play dead, fuck the Blackwood bitches.

I give my grandfather a hug as he makes his way out

the door. Down at the end of the driveway is a very dark looking SUV. It's heavily tinted barely allowing me to make out the silhouettes of the men inside. Let's not even start on the other vehicles that are lining the street, black SUVs just spell danger.

"One last thing Avery, I have a surprise for you in the next few days. You'll know it as soon as you see it." He gives me a wink as he makes his way to the back door of the SUV and gets inside.

I, on the other hand, make my way to the couch and plop down on it, then I reach and take out my phone.

Me: it was just some food that I ordered for dinner. I totally spaced it out but I'm going to eat now. I'll see you in the morning.

Tate: see ya tomorrow.

I knew halfway through my grandfather's visit that I won't be able to tell Tate anything, it would put her and me in a shit ton of danger, if she accidentally slipped.

Hopefully soon I'll be able to let her know everything that happened without both of us getting whacked. I just pray that she doesn't find out before I get to tell her, and never talks to me again.

MONDAY COMES AND GOES AS EXPECTED, NONE OF THE other students or Asher have relented. Even though I tell myself over and over again eventually they'll get bored, I'm not so sure. It was funny at first, even slightly entertaining, now it's just downright annoying. I'm going to start throwing punches, then I'll find myself kicked out of this damn forsaken school. That's all I need to happen now.

Tuesday is the day I'll always remember, the day that changed everything, at least for the better. That's what I thought, but I've never been so wrong.

At least lunch isn't as bad as the rest of the day's been, after everyone leaves us alone while we eat. Don't get me wrong, we still get the occasional snide comment or a rolled-up napkin, but it's nothing we can't handle.

I wonder if I mentioned to my grandfather that I'm being bullied, and if I stick up for myself, by sticking up I mean beat the shit out of, if he can smooth it over with the Dean, or at least Arya and Garrett can.

Once I start throwing a few punches people will definitely leave me alone. Who the hell wants to get punched, especially by a girl with a good right hook? I laugh as Tate gives me a weird look probably wondering if I've gone crazy.

Our peace and quiet is short-lived, Asher comes over to the table by himself. He sits down right in front of me and looks over at Tate and says, "leave."

I know she wants to say something smart, but she can't so my best friend, my lifeline, gets up and walks over to Asher's table and sits next to Liam and Carter. Nobody says anything, the whole damn cafeteria is focused on us.

"Why won't you leave?" He growls out.

"You thought of me as weak, huh?" I'm playing around. I don't think he's going to do anything right now, by himself, at least I hope he isn't.

He sighs and runs his hand through his hair. Even though he has a look of hate on his face, Asher is checking me out in a whole new light. "I did, but now all I think of you is stupid. Why won't you leave? What else needs to happen to get my point across, that I don't want you here?"

I raise my voice to where it's barely noticeable. "How do I get my point across to you that I don't give a shit what you want?"

He reaches across the table and grabs my hand and squeezes, not painful to where it hurts but enough to get my attention. "Let's go somewhere, we can quickly solve this issue, Avery." The lust is pouring off him in waves.

I throw my head back and laugh, so hard it hurts. It echoes out across the cafeteria causing others to chuckle with me. Tate's face is red and she's laughing as hard as I am, with tears coming down her face.

I have no idea how else to get my point across to the insolent bastard who doesn't understand or can't take no for an answer. I gather my belongings and stand up. Taking one last gulp of my fountain drink right before I dump the rest of it all over his head. The whole cafeteria can't keep what just happened to themselves even with possible repercussions, they howl in laughter, too. Maybe Asher is not as big and bad as he thought.

Asher stands up, his hands fisted at his side. I've never seen a more hateful look from somebody, anger is embedded in his soul as he looks at me with disgust.

A chair slides against the linoleum floor, making the squeak I hate so much, causing me to cringe. I know it's probably Tate getting ready to run over here to protect me. Asher takes my cringe as me being submissive, being scared and ready to bow down so he'll just leave me the fuck alone and won't hurt me anymore.

If he was a girl or I was a man, I can guarantee we'd both be swinging. The look on his face is pure hatred. It tells me he wouldn't mind laying me out right now. Most of the students and staff in here hopefully still have their humanity. Even I don't think a Mancini would get away with punching a female. Maybe I should just keep going at him, so he's got no choice. Then after he's kicked out I would actually find some freedom in this god-forsaken school.

The door to the cafeteria opens, it's so loud in this quiet space it makes all of us detour our attention.

When I see who's at the entrance to the cafeteria walking in like the bad ass bitch he is, I scream, I downright literally fucking scream.

This causes Asher to stumble backwards and look between me and the guy at the entrance to the cafeteria.

Even though I'm standing up my chair is right behind me, I move back letting the bastard fall to the floor. I can't run fast enough to the front door.

A smile that actually reaches the eyes of the unidentified stranger smiles back at me.

I can't get to him fast enough. "Mario!" I cry out as my whole-body barrels into his. His arms go around my waist and lifts me up. I wrap my legs around his hips to keep me from falling. I hug the shit out of one of my lifelong friends. Mario's been there for me all of my life. I wonder if he knew that my grandfather was alive, he does work for the Romano's. But who fucking cares, he's here now.

"Are you going to get down? Or are you going to just

keep squeezing me with your legs of death till I fall over?"
I laugh as Mario slowly lets me slide down to the floor.

I glance around the cafeteria forgetting where we were
for a minute. Students keep turning their attention
between us and Asher. Over half of them even have their
mouths open, including Paisley and her bitches. Liam and
Carter are laughing their asses off, while Walker and
Noah just sit with the same shocked expression as
everyone else.

Mario Bianchi is definitely someone to look at, the
man is a walking Adonis.

The one I should have worried about was *him.* Asher
was only mad a second ago, but that doesn't even compare
to the way he's looking at me right now. His face is bright
red and his hands are clenched even tighter, probably
bleeding. He's heading in this direction, thankfully his
crew physically blocks him from coming towards us.

For some reason I feel guilty, not like, take that motherfucker I got somebody else, but like I'm betraying him
somehow. He would've known had I left, I would have
ended up fucking somebody else. Well shit, maybe he
knew I wouldn't leave. Maybe it was his plan the whole
time to fuck me and then we'd go back to our normal way.

Funny thing is that Mario and I are not that way, we've
been friends since we were born, he's like my brother.

The way he's looking at me right now is escalating his
anger. If we were in a room by ourselves, I know he'd fuck
me or put a bullet in my head. I wasn't that nervous before
but for some reason I am now.

"Come on, let's go," Mario says as he grabs my hand
leading me from the cafeteria. It doesn't take a genius

looking at the situation to figure out what's going on, but at least he's here with me.

I'm able to sneak one more glance at everybody. My main focus is to see what Tate looks like, and happily my best friend is grinning ear-to-ear, the smile is definitely shining through.

Man, I'm going to have to talk to her about everything now, especially since she can't take her eyes off the guy standing next to me. Her and Mario would make an awesome couple.

CHAPTER 20

ASHER

I know my hands are bleeding from how hard I've been fisting them at my sides. Who the fuck is this douche with Avery, and why in the hell does he have his hands all over her?

Not of my own doing but for some reason my body just starts to gravitate towards her. Even though I don't know who this guy is, I don't even care if it's her freaking brother, she doesn't have one, I checked. I don't want anybody else's hands-on Avery except for mine.

Is this some kind of game? Is she trying to get a rise out of me by doing this, because it's definitely fucking working. She knows how much I want her, and she has the audacity to bring somebody else in that doesn't even go to the school.

I relax my body, letting the blood flow through my fingers. There is no way that Avery could be with this dude, he's a freaking preppy college boy. Granted, I don't even know exactly what she goes for, but when she's around me I know the type that she likes and this dick sure isn't it.

Before any other thoughts can conjure in my mind, or my body can move in her direction, I'm forcefully grabbed from both sides and led out of the cafeteria.

"Really?" I don't say anything else at my friends, I just let them drag me away. It's probably a good idea we're leaving, who knows what I would have done, especially if he touched her or even kissed her.

"Damn man, you've got it bad," Liam says laughing. "God I wish fucking Doppler was here to see this."

I shake my head, Doppler would be on the fucking cafeteria floor laughing his ass off if he could see this right now. He's still going to end up laughing when these dicks I call friends end up telling him. Nothing I can do, he knows I do have a freakish obsession with this girl.

I try to turn my head back and look, but my view is blocked as my friends keep pushing me out the door.

"Strip club again?" I ask a little bit more eagerly than normal. There's nothing I can fucking do right now about Avery, except land my ass in jail.

"No," Liam snaps, he has more to say but he's probably remembering I'm still his boss. "You've missed seven classes, if you keep ditching you ain't going to graduate."

Oh yeah, there's that, too. It'd be better if Avery was in my next class but she's not. I wonder what her and that douchebag are doing right now.

As soon as the thought goes through my head my body immediately turns and stomps back towards the cafeteria. Luckily for me, I only make it a few steps before I'm swung around and led in the direction of class.

"Dammit," I scream as my fist goes flying into the lockers by my next class causing it to cave in.

The students that are in my general vicinity slowly move themselves away from me. At least none of them flat-out run, I wouldn't have cared if they did.

Luckily for me my guys have my back, literally, as they push me into my next class. I was able to make it through the rest of the day. I would like to say that I focused on my studies and concentrated on the teachers, but all I could think about was Avery.

Right when the last bell rang to let out, I was out of my chair bypassing my locker and going out the front door. I wanted to be able to confront her and ask who this dick head is. If I had anything to say about it, she wasn't getting away before I found out.

I smirk as I notice the guys follow me out a couple minutes later, damn, all four of them.

Each of them are thinking something different, their thoughts are written all over their face. Walker and Noah have to keep pushing their lips together from busting out laughing. Liam smirks every now and then, but it's Carter that I keep looking at. His straight-faced look of annoyance plus disgust never changes. He's not one to wait for a woman, this whole thing must seem strange to him.

If he were in my shoes he probably would have went over and decked the guy, actually we would've grabbed him also. I chuckle under my breath.

A Porsche Cayenne parks over by the exit to the doors. Tate and Avery choose that time to walk out. When Avery spots the dickhead in the car she fucking skips, yes skips, over to him, and throws her arms around him for another hug. Lucky for both of them he didn't kiss her.

She doesn't even look in our direction. I know she can feel me glaring. I just wish she'd look over here. My eyes and my face say everything I'm feeling. I'm not feeling very grand right now.

Doppler comes and stands next to us. The guy's been waiting in one of the guard cars like he does every day until we get out of school.

I glare at him knowing what he's going to say before he does. No matter what I do though, as soon as his eyes connect on the situation with Avery and the guy she's with, he busts out laughing. The dickhead is laughing so loud that he goes back over and sits in the car. I swear I saw the fucker wiping his eyes. I'm never going to live this down.

"Let's go," I snap out. There's no reason to stay here and prolong this, besides, I need to figure out who this fucker is. I lift my cell phone and snap a couple shots, thankfully nobody sees me doing this.

I'm determined to figure out who this asshole is, maybe I can get a fucking name.

On the ride back the guys talk and banter between each other. I guess there's supposed to be a huge party at the end of the week, and they all want to go. These dick-heads love every new school year, because of all the new freshmen that come in, eager and willing to do anything to please an upperclassman. If they get in with the right group, they're set for the rest of their school years.

When we get back to the house I look around for Devon. I sent him a message before we left the school to meet us here. The bitch likes to work from home or the rented-out condo I'm paying for, for him.

The front door isn't even locked as I throw it open making my way towards the kitchen. Fucking Devon is in there with a bowl of cereal, not just a regular bowl, but one of those salad bowls and using a gallon of my fucking milk.

I set my phone down in front of him. "Find out who this fucking dick is, right away."

Devon nods as he sits up straight in his seat and grabs the phone, looking at the picture.

I get my own glass of milk as he goes through tapping on the screen, most likely sending it to himself or maybe he's able to figure out who he is from there.

All of us sit down and have an after-school snack, I smirk to myself. It's like we're freaking ten years old. We ran home from school to grab the Cheetos and plant our ass in front of the TV.

It doesn't take too long for Devon to figure out who it is, maybe ten minutes max, and that's only going on a picture alone. The picture is shit, grainy and far away.

"Mario Bianchi," Devon says as he takes his dishes over to the sink. Sometimes we wash them, but usually we just leave them for Tate to do, yeah we're assholes.

"Find out everything you can on him as soon as possible. I would like to know the dickhead that I'm dealing with." I pause for a minute and then it hits me. "Bianchi is one of the bigger families on the East Coast, why the fuck is he here to see Avery?"

I tried to find something to occupy my time, but of course it never works out that way. I pace for what seems like hours, but it was probably only minutes before Devon came back down.

Devon is the family analyst, he's been with our company for a while now. He's closer to me than with Armani and Rocco. I know he can't stand those dick bags any more than I can. With me being in charge, I keep Devon with me wherever I go.

If another family decided to attack us and break into the house, Devon would still be able to help us, even though he's lanky as fuck. Everybody in the family has to go through a rigorous training session, even the house-keepers.

Yeah, I also thought it was the stupidest thing I heard when I was younger, but it makes sense, especially after a bunch of men broke into the New York compound. We didn't have that many people stationed there at the time.

Everybody was woken up including the housekeepers. Fuck, some of them fight better than my own damn guys do. One of the sous chefs, I offered him a job as a guard, and he laughed. Said hell no, he'd rather be cooking and using knives, than sparring and using guns.

When you're fighting for any reason, all you can do is use what's readily available, and that just happened to be the workers. If another family comes into the house to do that, they're not going to just walk by the workers and leave them alone. No, they're going to take out everybody, no witnesses. The ones that are more advanced will also hit the cameras and get rid of any trace of them being there.

The smarter families like ours have multiple systems in place. We don't just have one camera company protecting our compound, no, we have another system setup, one that Devon designed, it's hidden well from other security companies.

"Asher," Devon says yanking me out of my thoughts. He's got a thick file in his hands, that must be everything on Avery.

I don't grab it from him yet, I stare at his face, his tortured face. Something's not right, this isn't looking good at all.

Devon doesn't say anything as he places the file right in front of me. He walks away before I even have a chance to open it.

For the next hour I go through the file in complete and utter shock. I keep looking up, expecting the other guys and Devon to be standing around me laughing at this joke they pulled.

But apparently, this whole time, the joke's been on me.

CHAPTER 21

AVERY

Last night I sent a message to Tate letting her know that she didn't have to pick me up anymore.

She sent me a message back letting me know I can start picking her up. I laughed. She's right, we can even car pool or some days go by ourselves.

I practically skip out the front door to my new car. I knew exactly what I wanted yesterday. Even Mario laughed when he saw where I was going, and what I wanted to buy.

I unlock the doors on my new Dodge Ram truck, even though it's a 2020 if I would've waited a few more months I could have gotten the 2021.

This is the vehicle I wanted, mainly because my dad drove one for so long. Even as a kid all I remember my dad ever having is a Dodge. I knew I would feel closer to him by buying this. When I took it for a test drive my decision was made.

Since I'm paying cash, we should've been at the auto

place for about an hour, I made a mistake in bringing Mario. There was one salesman there that he could not take his eyes off. He would practically drool every time this man walked by.

Oh yeah, Mario is as gay as they come, and one of my lifelong friends. It took most his life, but about a year ago he finally opened up to his parents and thank God they were okay with it. If they were not okay with it, they probably would have just ended him or sent him far away to a reform school for gays or some stupid shit like that.

The only stipulation they have is when on the East Coast he cannot be gay, that's a weakness to the families, which of course is total bullshit. They just don't want a gay man to beat the shit out of one of them. I guess they feel better if it's from a straight man.

I got the brown with a chrome style finish on my truck. The color has nothing to do with anything, that's just something I wanted.

Having a bigger truck does make me feel more invincible, like I've got bigger balls. If one of those bitches at school gives me shit, I'll just run over their little BMW's, hopefully with them still in it.

On the drive to school my mind goes back to the day before seeing Asher. He was freaking fuming when he saw me with Mario.

I quickly averted my gaze when all of his friends started to drag him away in another direction. If he only realized how gay Mario was.

Mario picked up on them right when we were in the cafeteria. As soon as we hit the parking lot the barrage of questions started spilling from his mouth.

I explained everything I could. We were in the car for a while before we got out, I wanted Mario to know the whole situation.

I wasn't expecting him to growl out. "What the fuck is wrong with you? Screw that God of a man and get it out of your system, and then call me and tell me everything."

I start laughing again. I'm glad he's going to be here for a little bit before he's got to go back. Grandpa asked him as a favor to check up on me.

I have no doubt that he accepted instantly, my friend is a gay slut. Beaches and bars in California are going to be his playground for the whole time he's here.

I want to hang out with Mario, I miss him, so I'll definitely go wherever he's going. It's always fun when we get together.

Sadly enough, my thoughts revert back to Asher. At first he looked crushed, like how could I do this to him, but in the next instant he was pissed, beyond pissed.

I don't want him to be hurt or mad. I definitely don't want him to take it out on me later, which I know is coming. He doesn't know who Mario is, that's why he probably didn't approach. I start laughing really loud as the driver at the light next to me just gives me a weird look and turns back ahead. The only reason Asher didn't come in after me is because his friends were holding him back. Mario genuinely believes things are going to come to a head soon enough between us.

Don't get me wrong, I haven't forgotten about the fact I still have to deal with the Adonis, but what happens after that? I just wish I knew.

Luckily for me I don't have to find out yet. Asher and

his guys haven't shown up for school, which I find a little awkward. Maybe he had to head back to New York for business, who knows.

I don't know what I expected not seeing him today. I'm excited, but also a little bit down. For some reason I just want to see his annoyed, pissed off, I hate the world face, today.

For the first time this year Tate has actually beat me to the cafeteria. She's already got her food and her happy ass is sitting down at the table. I need to rectify that, not her happy ass, her very miserable ass. Her face screams I'm a Mancini and I hate my life.

I always tell her just to run. If she's so miserable here, why is she staying? Deep down inside I know the answer, she's staying for somebody. I have a feeling it's the person who owns the house. I just wish she would trust me enough to tell me.

I want to hit my head against the wall by the cafeteria door. I shouldn't even consider being upset that I still don't know all of her secrets when I'm definitely holding a doozy of my own.

I can't find the perfect time or place to tell her. I want her to know, but it could put my life in danger. I seriously doubt she's going to go run to Asher or even the other Mancini's and let them know who I am.

"Hey," I say as I sit down with five tacos I loaded on my plate, yes five tacos. It's taco day at school.

"Hey yourself. So, tell me more about this Mario guy." Tate says as she bats her eyelashes at me.

Even though Mario is gay, he is still fucking hot. Even when the women learn that he's gay, it doesn't sway them at all. It's the same old saying that if they're good enough sexually that they'll be able to convert a gay man.

"He's as gay as they come," I say before I stuff my first taco in my mouth, not all of it, but if my mouth was big enough I sure as hell would.

Tate stops eating. "Really? I would have never thought that. He's a fucking beefcake and his hair, don't even get me started on his blue eyes. Fuck, why are all the good ones taken or gay?"

This time I really start laughing. I just wish Mario could hear what she said.

"This is kind of fun actually," Tate says as she looks at me with sparkling eyes. "I know you noticed how upset Asher was with Mario's hands all over you. I think you should play this for a while."

My eyes are wide as I just look at her. "There is no way in hell I see that happening, someone would die."

Tate smiles as she looks at me, something is up her sleeve. "Just think, Asher can be all broody and stompy towards you. But right when he gets to his table, the cafeteria doors explode open as Mario casually struts ever so slowly right to where you're sitting. Asher is in too much shock to do anything when Mario comes up, yanks you from your chair and devours you with his mouth." She sighs in content and goes back to her food.

I'm full out laughing again, people must either think I'm drunk or on drugs. This has been a really good day so far.

Of course, I always speak too soon. Asher pulls out the chair right next to me and sits down, giving me a wink.

He looks over to Tate and snaps, "leave."

Tate frantically looks between us. I know she can't disobey the hierarchy of the family, but she doesn't want to leave her friend, either.

"I'll be fine, we're in the middle of the cafeteria, lots of people around," I say hoping that's true. "But honestly, what can he do that he hasn't done before? He just wants to get on my nerves or tell me to fuck him again." I'm speaking to Tate but looking at Asher.

His crew stands up in front of the table with their backs to us, facing everybody in the cafeteria. Of course, this makes everybody in the cafeteria stop and stare, wondering what's going on. They could've just walked away or sat down on the other side. This is starting to look like I'm about to get a cap in my ass.

Asher moves closer, wraps his arm over my shoulder, then he bends down to whisper in my ear. "I'm going to have so much fun fucking you Avery."

I roll my eyes and try to push the body of cement away from me, of course he doesn't even budge.

"Are we seriously on this shit again, Asher? I'm not going to fuck you. I'm not going to be anything to you. Let this go, please." I add the last part for emphasis, even though I seriously doubt it will help with anything.

"I think you and I are going to have a lot of fun together, more fun than you can ever dream of." He states as he twirls a piece of my hair.

"I've had enough of this." I don't want to keep doing this, but unfortunately I'm stuck in this fucking school. Go me.

I stand up and grab my tray. I don't make it that far

before Asher whispers loud enough for me to hear. "Sit the fuck down *Mila*, we need to talk."

My tray smacks against the table, since I released it in shock, not even realizing it was in my hands. My eyes widen as my butt plops back into the seat. My mouth is open in shock as Asher uses his index finger under my chin, closing one of my orifices, one I'm fairly sure he wants.

The school bell rings, as the students jump up to make it to their class in time. Not me, I'm still stuck in this chair with my eyes wide open unable to move.

"I'll see you tonight, *Avery*." At least he used the name I prefer. I try to say something as he holds up his hand and threatens. "Or everyone, mainly Luca, might find out your real name."

Oh God, what's going to happen now? I think to myself watching Asher walk away. "I am completely fucked."

ABOUT THE AUTHOR

K.J. currently lives in New England with her Husband and children. (Boys, yep K.J. has a houseful of boys!) There's never a dull moment. She has two large dogs and two asshole cats to add to the Family. Years ago, K. J. worked as an engineer with IBM. Once married she decided to be a stay-at-home Mom, a decision she's never regretted.

K.J. loves to read and write dark, suspenseful romance. When she's not reading or writing you can find her in the garden or snuggled up with her Family on the couch for movie night.

To keep in touch click below, or sign up for my Newsletter.

ALSO BY K.J. THOMAS

Deceived by Lies: (Moretti Siblings Book 1)

Fighting Back: (Moretti Siblings Book 2)

No Escape: (Moretti Siblings Book 3)

Sweet Surrender: (Moretti Siblings Book 4)

Not Giving up: A Bully Romance: (Ridgeside High Book 1)

Pushed Away: A Bully Romance: (Ridgeside High Book 2)

Cruel Games: A Bully Romance: (Ridgeside High Book 3)

One More Day: A Bully Romance: (Ridgeside High Book 4)

Hiding from Monsters: A High School Bully Romance: (Blackwood Academy Book 1)

Running from Monsters: A High School Bully Romance: (Blackwood Academy Book 2)

ACKNOWLEDGMENTS

I want to sincerely let my Husband, kids and Nana know how much I appreciate them, not for what they've done during my writing of these books, but what they've endured. I was 100% book focused and nothing else. I love you guys!

CPSIA information can be obtained
at www.ICGtesting.com
Printed in the USA
BVHW091922220922
647758BV00004B/748